"We're married."

"It was a mistake!" Caroline insisted.

"Not as far as I'm concerned."

"I'll have it annulled," she threatened.

Paul's grin was wide and cynical. "After last night?"

Her cheeks flamed even hotter. So something *had* happened. "I have no intention of staying married to you. Good heavens, I don't even know you!"

"You'll have plenty of time for that later."

"Later? I'm not staying here a second longer than necessary. There's been a terrible mistake, and I want out before it gets even worse...."

Dear Reader:

The spirit of the Silhouette Romance Homecoming Celebration lives on as each month we bring you six books by continuing stars!

And we have a galaxy of stars planned for 1988. In the coming months, we're publishing romances by many of your favorite authors such as Annette Broadrick, Sondra Stanford and Brittany Young. Beginning in January, Debbie Macomber has written a trilogy designed to cure any midwinter blues. And that's not all—during the summer, Diana Palmer presents her most engaging heros and heroines in a trilogy that will be sure to capture your heart.

Your response to these authors and other authors of Silhouette Romances has served as a touchstone for us, and we're pleased to bring you more books with Silhouette's distinctive medley of charm, wit and—above all—romance.

I hope you enjoy this book and the many stories to come. Come home to romance—for always!

Sincerely,

Tara Hughes
Senior Editor
Silhouette Books

DEBBIE MACOMBER

Mail-Order Bride

Published by Silhouette Books New York

America's Publisher of Contemporary Romance

To
Ron and Marion Cowden
Beloved New Zealand Friends
and to
The Kiwi Magic

SILHOUETTE BOOKS
300 E. 42nd St., New York, N.Y. 10017

Copyright © 1987 by Debbie Macomber

ISBN: 0-373-08539-7

First Silhouette Books printing November 1987

America's Publisher of Contemporary Romance

Printed in the U.S.A.

Books by Debbie Macomber

Silhouette Romance

Silhouette Special Edition

DEBBIE MACOMBER

has quickly become one of Silhouette's most prolific authors. As a wife and mother of four, she not only manages to keep her family happy, but she also keeps her publisher and readers happy with each book she writes.

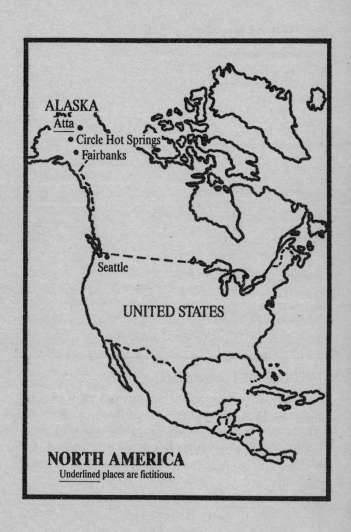

ALASKA
Atta
● Circle Hot Springs
● Fairbanks

Seattle

UNITED STATES

NORTH AMERICA
Underlined places are fictitious.

Prologue

I'm so dreadfully worried about dear Caroline," Ethel Myers murmured thoughtfully, sipping her tea from the dainty porcelain cup. Her fingers clutched a delicate lace-trimmed handkerchief and when a tiny droplet of moisture formed in the corner of her eye, she dabbed it gently. "Sister, I do believe the brew is much stronger today."

"Yes," Mabel admitted gingerly. "But remember what Father said about the brew enhancing one's ability to solve problems."

"And we must do something to help Caroline."

Mabel sighed and sadly shook her head. "Perhaps if you and I had married suitable gentlemen all those years ago."

"Oh yes, if we'd married then maybe we'd know how to help that sweet, sweet child." Ethel's faded blue eyes brightened momentarily. "You do remember that George Guettermann once asked for my hand."

"As I recall, Mother was quite impressed with him."

The slender shoulders sagged slightly. "But Father was suspicious from the first."

Mabel sighed heavily. "Mr. Guettermann did cut such a dashing figure."

A wistful look marked Ethel's fragile features. "If only he hadn't already been married."

"The scoundrel!"

"We must learn to forgive him, Sister."

Mabel nodded and lifted the steaming pot of brew. "I was thinking of Caroline's young man. Another cup, Sister?"

"Oh dear, should we?" Ethel's fingers flew to her mouth to smother a loud hiccup, and she had the good grace to look embarrassed.

"We must find a way to help her."

"Poor, poor Caroline." Ethel agreed as Mabel filled the cup to the bright gold rim.

"There was something in his eyes."

"George?"

"No, Sister. Caroline's young man."

"I do agree, there was indeed something about his eyes." Ethel took another sip of tea and lightly patted her breast at the strength of their father's special recipe. "Sister, the brew..."

"We must think!"

"Oh yes, I do agree. Think. We must help dear, dear Caroline."

"If only her mother were alive."

"Or grandmother."

"Grandmother?"

"Great-great-grandmother, perhaps. She would know what to do to help Caroline. You know how her great-great-grandmother frowned on the courting; she said it simply wasn't necessary."

"Grandmother would. Asa Mercer brought her to Seattle with the other mail-order brides and she and Grandfather knew each other less than twenty-four hours before they married."

"A courtship wasn't necessary and they were so very happy."

"Very happy indeed and very compatible."

"With twelve children they must have agreed quite nicely," Ethel said, and giggled delightedly.

"It's such a shame marriages aren't arranged these days," Mabel said thoughtfully, taking another long sip of the tea.

"If only we could find Caroline a husband."

"But, Sister..." Mabel was doubtful. For over fifty years they'd been unable to locate husbands of their own. It was unreasonable to expect to come up with one for their beloved niece.

Ethel's hand shook as she lowered the fragile cup to the saucer. "Sister, Sister. I do believe I have the solution," her voice wavered with excitement as she reached for the morning paper.

"Yes?"

"Our own Caroline will be a mail-order bride."

Mabel looked doubtful. "But things aren't done like that in this day and age."

Ethel fumbled with the printed pages until she located the classified section. She folded back the unwieldy page and pointed to the personal column. "Here, read this."

Mabel read the ad aloud, her voice trembling. "Wanted—Wife for thirty-two-year-old Alaskan male. Send picture. Transportation provided." The advertisement listed the name of Paul Trevor and a box number.

"But, Sister, do we dare?"

"We must. Caroline is so desperately unhappy."

"And she did have the opportunity to select a husband of her own."

"And the beast left her standing at the altar."

"The scoundrel!"

"We mustn't tell her, of course."

"Oh no, we can't let her know. Our Caroline would object most strenuously."

"Sister, I do believe the brew helped."

"Indeed! Another cup?"

Ethel lifted her cup and her older sister automatically refilled it. A small smile of satisfaction lifted the edges of her soft mouth. "Father's recipe was most beneficial."

"It always is, Sister."

"Oh yes, indeed."

Chapter One

The roaring sound of the jet sliced through the air as the Boeing 767 prepared to land at the Seattle-Tacoma International Airport. Caroline Myers watched the thick tires bounce over the runway with the realization that she would soon depart Seattle for unknown adventures in Alaska.

"Do you have everything, dear?" Mabel asked her niece for the third time in as many minutes.

"Aunt Ethel, Aunt Mabel, please—I cannot allow you to do this."

"Nonsense," Ethel said with an imperceptible cluck. "This vacation is our gift to you."

"But Alaska in October?"

"It's lovely, dear heart. I promise."

"Yes, lovely," Ethel agreed, doing her best to hide a soft smile. "And we have the nicest surprise waiting for you."

Caroline stared suspiciously at her two maiden aunts. Mischief danced in their sparkling blue eyes. At sixty-nine and seventy, they were her only living relatives in Seattle, and she loved them dearly.

"But this trip is too much."

"Nonsense."

"Hurry, dear, or you'll miss your plane."

"One question?"

Ethel and Mabel exchanged fleeting glances. "Yes?"

"Why the blood tests? I didn't know anything like that was necessary for travel within the United States."

Mabel paused to clear her throat, wildly casting her eyes about the terminal. "It's something new."

"A gubernatorial decision, I...I believe," Ethel stammered.

"Now take this," Mabel instructed, handing her niece a neatly packed wicker basket. "We filled a thermos with Father's special tea in case you need it."

"I just may," Caroline said, doing her utmost to swallow a chuckle. She'd been eighteen when she'd first discovered the potency of her great-grandfather's special recipe.

"And do write."

"Of course. I'll send a postcard every day." Caroline kissed both aunts on the cheek and hugged them gently. Ethel sniffled and Mabel cast her a look of sisterly displeasure. Again Caroline grinned. Her two great-aunts had been a constant delight for all of her life. They were charming, loving and thoroughly enchanting. The two had done everything they could to cheer her after Larry's defection. The sudden memory of the man she had loved with such intensity produced a fresh wave of pain that threatened to wash away the pleasure of this moment.

Ethel sniffled again. "We shall miss you dreadfully," she announced, glaring at her sister.

Caroline threw back her head and laughed aloud. Her long blond hair fell like a cascading river down the middle of her back. "I'm only going to be gone a week." Again Ethel's and Mabel's eyes avoided hers and Caroline wondered what little game they were playing.

"But a week seems so very long."

"You have your ticket?" Mabel asked hurriedly.

"Right here." Caroline patted the side of her purse.

"Remember, a nice young man will be meeting you in Fairbanks."

"Right," Caroline said, eyes twinkling. Her aunts had gone over the details of this vacation a minimum of fifty times. "And he's taking me to . . ."

"Atta," the great-aunts chimed, bobbing their heads in unison.

"From there, I'll be met by . . ."

"Paul Trevor." Ethel and Mabel shared a silly grin.

"Right, Paul Trevor." Caroline studied her aunts surreptitiously. If she didn't know better, she'd think they had something up their sleeves. For days, the two of them had been acting like giddy teenagers, whispering and giggling behind her back. Caroline had objected to this vacation from the first. Alaska in early

October wouldn't have been her first choice; she wouldn't have argued nearly as strenuously had they suggested Hawaii, but her two aunts had been so insistent that Alaska was the best place for her that Caroline had finally agreed. This was their unselfish gift to her in an effort to heal a broken heart, and she wasn't about to ruin it by being stubborn. She couldn't bear to inform them that it would take a whole lot more than a trip north for her heart to mend.

The flight attendant announced that the plane was now boarding and called off the number of Caroline's row. Caroline hugged her aunts and secured her purse strap over her shoulder.

"Do be happy, dear," Ethel said, pressing her frilly lace handkerchief under her nose. Her eyes misted with emotion.

Mabel's voice seemed strained as she echoed her sister's words and clenched Caroline's free hand. "Happiness, child. Much, much happiness."

Shaking her head at the strange behavior of the two, Caroline entered the long, narrow jetway that led to the belly of the Boeing 767. The flight attendant directed her to the first-class section, and, again, Caroline had cause to consider how her aunts could possibly afford this trip. She clipped the seat belt into place and pressed the recliner button, leaning as far back in the wide seat as possible.

From inside the airport, Ethel and Mabel stood looking at the sleek body of the aircraft that would carry away their beloved niece.

"It's fate, Sister," Mabel said softly.

"Oh, indeed. Paul Trevor chose her over all those other women."

"He sounds like such a good man."

"And so handsome."

"Only he wrote that he has a beard now. Does Caroline like men with beards?"

Ethel gently shook her head. "I really couldn't say."

"She'll grow to love him."

"Oh yes. Given time, she'll be very happy with Paul."

"Perhaps she'll be as compatible with him as Grandmother was with Grandfather."

"Twelve children. Oh, Sister, what a delightful thought." Ethel pressed her gloved hands to her rosy cheeks and smiled through the misting tears.

Doubts vanished and the two shared a brilliant smile before turning away.

"We did our best for her," Mabel stated happily. "Her mother would have been proud."

"Her great-great-grandmother, too," Ethel said, and the two giggled with pure delight, causing several curious glances to be cast in their direction.

Caroline slept for most of the night flight to Fairbanks. She was exhausted from a hectic week at the office. As a private nurse for Dr. Kenneth James, an internist, she often put in long days and odd hours. Dr. James gave her the week off without a complaint and then, on Friday morning, shook her hand and wished her much happiness. Now that she thought about it, Caroline found his words puzzling. One didn't find happiness on a vacation. Happiness was the result of a satisfactory relationship. Like hers and Larry's... His name drifted with such ease into her mind that Caroline shook her head in an effort to free her thoughts.

Straightening in her seat, she noted that the cabin lights were dimmed. The only other passenger in the first-class section was sleeping, and the two attendants were drinking coffee in the front cabin. When one of them noticed that Caroline was awake, the attractive woman approached her.

"You missed the meal. Would you care to eat something now?"

Caroline shook her head. "No, thanks."

The tall brunette responded with a slight nod and returned to her coffee. Caroline viewed the trim body as she walked away. The flight attendant was more the type of woman Larry should marry, she mused, unable to keep her thoughts from wandering to her former fiancé. She'd known from the beginning how completely dissimilar Larry's and her tastes ran. Larry liked late, late nights and breakfast in bed while she was a morning person, eager for each new day. Caroline enjoyed the outdoor life: hiking, camping, boating. Larry's idea of roughing it was doing without valet service. She liked cornflakes with chocolate syrup poured over the top, milk mixed with Pepsi, and spaghetti for breakfast. Larry much preferred formal dinners with nothing more exotic than meat and potatoes. But they'd loved each other enough to believe they could overcome their differences and learn to compromise. *She* had loved *him*, Caroline corrected herself. At the last minute, Larry had buckled under to his doubts and had sent his witless brother to contact her an hour before the wedding ceremony. Humiliation engulfed her, threatening to smother her.

For the first week, Caroline hid from the world. Her two beloved aunts had hovered over her constantly, insisting that she eat and sleep, taking her temperature in case she'd worked herself into a case of the ague. Caroline assumed that the ague must be something dreadful and allowed them to fret over her. At the time, it would have taken more energy to assure them she was doing fine than to submit to their tender ministrations.

A month passed and Caroline gradually worked her way out of the heavy depression that had hung over her head like a constant thundercloud, threatening a fierce squall at any time. She smiled and laughed, but strongly suspected that her two maiden aunts were unconvinced. Every time she was with them, they stuck a thermometer under her tongue and shook their shiny gray heads with worried frowns.

Larry contacted her only once to stammer his regret and to apologize repeatedly. If she hadn't been so much in love with him, she might have been able to accept that he'd probably done them both a favor. Now there were whole hours when she didn't think about him, or hunger for information about him, or long to be held in his arms. Still, the thought of him with another woman was almost more than Caroline could tolerate, but given time she would learn to accept that as well.

This disaster with Larry had taught her that she possessed a far stronger constitution than she'd ever believed. She had been able to smile and hold her head high, and return to work a week after the aborted wedding. It hadn't been easy, but she'd done it with a calm maturity that surprised her. She was going to come out of this a much wiser, more discerning woman. Someday there would be a man who loved her enough to appreciate her sometimes wacky ways. When they fell in love and the time was right, she'd think about marriage again. But not for a long time, Caroline decided—not for a very long time.

As the plane approached the runway, Caroline gathered her things, preparing to disembark. Just as her aunts had promised, there was a man waiting for her in Fairbanks. She had no sooner walked off the plane than the middle-aged man with bushy eyebrows and a walrus mustache held up a piece of cardboard with her name printed across it in bold letters.

"Hello, I'm Caroline Myers," she told him, shifting the wicker basket from one hand to the other.

"Welcome to Alaska," he told her with a wide grin and offered his hand. "The name's John Morrison."

Caroline took it for a brisk shake. She liked him immediately. "Thank you, John."

The man continued to stare at her and rubbed the side of his square jaw. Slowly, he shook his head, and a sly grin courted the edges of his mouth. "Paul did all right for himself."

"Pardon?"

"Ah, nothing," John responded, shaking his head again. "I'm just surprised is all. I didn't expect him to come up with anyone half as attractive as you. I don't suppose you have a friend or two?"

Caroline hadn't the faintest idea what this burly bush pilot was getting at, or why he would be curious about her friends. Surely he'd flown more than one woman into the Alaskan interior. She was like any other tourist visiting Alaska for a one-week stay. She planned on getting plenty of rest and relaxation on the direct orders of her two maiden aunts. In addition, she hoped to sleep until noon every day, take invigorating walks and explore the magic of the tundra. Her aunts had mentioned Paul Trevor's name on several occasions and Caroline believed that they must have hired him as her guide. She wouldn't mind having someone show her the countryside. There was so much to see and do, and Caroline was ready for it all.

Once John had collected her suitcase, he directed her to the single-engine Cessna and helped her climb aboard.

"It won't be long now," he said, placing the earphones over his head and flipping several switches. He zipped up his fur-lined coat and glanced in her direction with a thick frown. Then the control tower issued instructions and John turned his attention to the radio. Once on the runway, the plane accelerated forward and was soon aiming for the clear, blue sky in a burst of power that had Caroline clenching her fingers together as if that alone would help to keep them airborne. She was accustomed to flying, but never in anything quite this small. In comparison to the wide-bodied jet, this Cessna seemed delicate and fragile.

"You might want to check some of those boxes back there." He jerked his head toward the large pile of sacks and cardboard boxes resting next to her suitcase at the rear of the plane.

"What should I be looking for?"

"A coat. It's going to get damn cold up here."

"All right." Caroline unhooked the seat belt and turned around to bend over the back of the padded cushion. She sorted through the sacks and found a variety of long underwear and flannel shirts.

"Paul's right about you needing this equipment. I hope the boots fit. I got the best available—fur-lined, naturally."

"Boots?"

"Lady, trust me. You're going to need them."

"I imagine they were expensive." She had a few traveler's checks with her, but if Paul Trevor expected her to pick up the tab on a complete winter wardrobe then he had another thought coming.

Caroline located the thick coat, but it was so bulky that she placed it over her knees and slipped her arms into a cozy flannel shirt.

"What did you bring with you?" John asked, eyeing the wicker basket at Caroline's feet.

"My two aunts sent along something to eat. They don't trust meals served on a commercial flight."

John's chuckle had a musical sound to it. "Smart woman."

Now that he'd mentioned the basket, Caroline discovered she was hungry. It'd been hours since she had last eaten, and her stomach growled as she lifted the wicker lid to discover one side loaded with thick sandwiches and the promised thermos. The second half of the basket contained a brightly wrapped gift.

Somewhat surprised, Caroline lifted the package and tore off the bright paper and ribbon. The paper-thin, sheer negligee with the fur-trimmed sleeves and hemline baffled her further.

John saw her blink in wonder and gave a loud laugh. "I see they included something to keep your neckline warm."

Caroline found his humor less than amusing and stuffed the gown back inside the basket. She'd never thought of her aunts as senile, but their recent behavior gave her cause to wonder.

She shared a thick turkey sandwich with John and listened while he spoke at length about Alaska. His love for this last frontier was apparent with every sentence. His running dialogue included a vivid description of the rolling tundra and varied wildlife.

"I have a feeling you're going to love it here."

"I like what little I've seen," Caroline agreed. She'd expected the land to be barren and harsh. It was that, but mingled in with the terrain was a subtle beauty, an elegance that instantly captured Caroline's heart.

"That's Denali over there," John told her. "She's the highest peak in North America."

"I thought McKinley was."

"Folks around here prefer to call her Denali."

"What's that?" Caroline pointed to the thin ribbon that stretched and wound its way aimlessly across the rugged countryside below.

"The Yukon River. She flows over two thousand miles from northwest Canada to the Bering Sea."

"I'm impressed."

"Is there anything you'd like to know about Paul?"

"Paul Trevor? Not really. Is there anything I should know?" Like her two aunts, John seemed to mention the other man's name at every opportunity.

He gave another merry chuckle. "Guess you'll be finding out everything about him soon enough."

"Right." She eyed him curiously. The way things were going, she'd be anxious to get a look at this man who insisted she have all this costly gear.

"He's a quiet man, but you'll grow accustomed to that."

"I usually chatter enough for two. I think we'll get along fine. Besides, I don't plan on being here that long."

John frowned. "I doubt that you'll ever get Paul to leave Alaska."

Caroline was offended by the brisk tone. "I don't have any intention of trying."

The amusement faded from John's rugged face as he checked the instruments on the front panel. "You aren't afraid of flying, are you?"

She hadn't thought about it much until he mentioned it. "Afraid? Why should I be afraid?"

"It looks like we may be headed into a bit of a storm. Nothing to worry about, mind you, if you aren't accustomed to a few jerks now and again. This could be a real roller coaster for a while."

"I'm fine." The sudden chill in the cabin caused Caroline to reach for the thermos. "My aunts make a mean cup of tea. Interested?"

"No, thanks." He focused his attention on the gauges and slipped his seat belt into place. Caroline mimicked his actions, her fingers trembling.

The first cup of the spiked tea brought a rush of warmth to her chilled arms, and when the plane pitched and heaved, Caroline refilled the plastic cup and gulped down a second. "Hey, this is fun," she said with a tiny laugh twenty minutes later. If the truth be known, she was frightened half out of her wits, but she put on a brave front and held on to the cup with both hands. Her aunts' tea was courage in a thermos.

By the time John announced they were within a half hour of Atta, Caroline's cheeks were a bright rosy hue and she was as warm as toast. As they made their descent, she peeked out the window at the uneven row of houses. A thick blanket of snow covered the ground and curling rings of smoke rose from a dozen chimneys.

"It's not much of a town, is it?"

"Around three hundred. Mostly Athabascans—they're Indians who were once nomadic, following caribou and other game. Once the white settlers arrived, they established permanent villages. Nowadays, they mostly hunt and fish. Once we get a bit closer you'll see a string of caribou hides drying in the sun."

"How interesting." Caroline knew that sounded trite, but she didn't know how else to comment.

"Paul's the only white man there."

"Oh."

"Naturally you'll be there now."

"What does Paul do?"

John gave her a curious stare. "I thought you would know. He keeps tabs on the pump station for the pipeline."

She brushed aside the soft, blond curl that fell over her face. "I thought he was a guide of some sort."

As the Cessna circled the village, Caroline saw what appeared to be tiny ants scurrying out of the houses. Several raised their arms high above their heads and waved. "They see us."

"They've probably spent days preparing for your arrival."

"How thoughtful." The village must only entertain a handful of tourists a year, she thought, and residents obviously went to a great deal of trouble to make sure that those who did arrive felt welcome. Caroline rubbed her eyes. It seemed the whole world was pitching and weaving. The people and the houses blurred together and she shook her head, hoping to gain some of her bearings. The thermos was empty; Caroline was more than a little intoxicated.

A glance at the darkening clouds produced a loud grumble from John. "It doesn't look like I'm going to be able to stick around for the reception."

"I'm sorry." John was probably a local hero. This welcoming party was likely to be as much in his honor as her own. By now it appeared that the entire village was outside pointing toward the sky and waving enthusiastically. "I don't see any runway."

"There isn't one."

"But..."

"There's enough of a clearing to make a decent landing. I've come down in a lot worse conditions."

Caroline's long nails cut into her palm. She didn't find his words all that reassuring. Why her aunts would choose such a remote village was beyond her.

This whole trip was turning into much more of an adventure than she'd ever dreamed.

As the plane descended, she closed her eyes until she felt the landing wheels bounce over the uneven ground. She was jostled, jolted and jarred, but was otherwise unscathed. Once they came to a complete stop, Caroline breathed again.

The single engine continued to purr as John unhooked his seat belt. "Go ahead and climb out. I'll hand you the gear."

Using her shoulder to pry open the airplane door, Caroline nearly fell to the snow in an effort to climb down gracefully. A gust of wind sobered her instantly. "Lordy, it's cold."

"Right, but Paul will warm you," John shouted enthusiastically over the engine's noise. He tossed out her suitcase and a large variety of boxes and sacks. "Good luck to you. I have a feeling you're the best thing to happen to Paul in a long while."

"Thanks." She stood in the middle of the supplies and blinked twice. "Aren't you coming with me?"

"No time. I've got to get out of here before this storm hits." He waved, shut the door and a minute later was taxiing away.

With a sense of disbelief, Caroline watched him leave. Already she could see a team of dogs pulling a large sled racing toward her. She waved on the off chance they couldn't see her. Again the earth seemed to shift beneath her feet, and she rubbed her eyes in an effort to maintain her balance. Good grief, just how much of that tea had she drunk? Apparently enough!

By the time the first dogsled arrived, she'd produced a synthetic smile. "Hello," she greeted and raised her hand, praying no one would guess that she was more than a little tipsy.

"Welcome."

The man who must be Paul Trevor walked toward her and handed her a small bouquet of flowers. He was tall and dark, and from what she could see of his bearded face, reasonably attractive. Untamed curls grew with rakish disregard across a wide, intelligent brow. His eyes were as blue as her own, and were deep and thoughtful. She had taken to John Morrison immediately, but Caroline wasn't sure that she would like this man. John had spoken of him with respect, and it was obvious that he was considered a leader among the villagers. But his intensity unnerved her. His eyes held the determination of a mule. Caroline wasn't about to let him intimidate her; however, now wasn't the time to say much of anything. Not when her tongue refused to cooperate with her brain.

"Thank you." Caroline smelled the flowers, expecting to savor the sweet scent of spring, only to have her nose tickled by the prickly needles. Startled, her eyes popped open.

"They've been dried."

"Oh." She felt like a fool. There weren't flowers in Atta this time of year. "Of course—they must be."

"Everything's ready if you are."

"Sure." Caroline assumed he was speaking of the welcoming reception.

The large group of natives quickly loaded her suitcase and the other boxes onto the sleds. Caroline took a step toward Paul and nearly stumbled. Again the ground pitched and heaved under her feet. She recognized it as the potency of the tea and not an earthquake, but for a moment she was confused. "I'm sorry," she murmured and shook her head. "I seem to be a bit unsteady."

Paul guided her to the dogsled. "It might be better if you sat." He pulled back the thick hide and helped her into the sled. The huge husky turned his head around to examine her and Caroline grinned sheepishly at the dog. "I don't weigh much," she told him, and giggled. Good grief, she was beginning to sound like her aunts.

The short trip into Atta took only a matter of minutes. Paul helped her out of the sled and led her into the long narrow building in the center of the village. Candles flickered all around the room. Tables filled with a wide variety of meats and other dishes lined the walls. A priest, Russian Orthodox, Caroline guessed, was dressed in a long gold robe. He smiled at her warmly and stepped forward to greet her, taking her hand in his.

"Welcome to Atta. I'm Father Nabokov."

"I'm pleased to meet you, Father." Caroline prayed that he didn't smell her aunts' brew on her breath.

"Are you hungry?" Paul had shed his thick coat and took hers. The force of his personality was defined in his stance. On meeting him, Caroline understood why both John and her two aunts had found occasion to mention Paul. His personality was forceful, but there was a gentleness to him as well, a tenderness he preferred to disguise.

"Hungry? No...not really," she replied tentatively, realizing that she was staring at him. Paul didn't seem to mind. For that matter, he appeared to be sizing her up as well, and from the lazy, sensual smile that spread from his mouth to his eyes, he appeared to like what he saw.

If Caroline could only have cleared her mind, she felt she might have been able to start up a witty conversation, but her thoughts were preoccupied with the noisy murmuring around her. It looked as though the entire village was crammed inside the meeting hall. Someone was playing music, but it wasn't on an instrument that Caroline recognized. A fiddle player joined the first man and the festive mood spread until everyone was laughing and singing. Several helped themselves to plates and heaped large amounts of food from the serving dishes.

"Perhaps it would be best if we started things now," Father Nabokov suggested. "It doesn't look like we'll be able to hold things up much longer."

"Do you mind?" Paul glanced toward Caroline.

"Not in the least. Why wait?" Nearly everyone was eating and drinking as it was, and she could see no reason to delay the party. Someone brought her a glass of champagne and Caroline drank it down in one big swallow. The room was warm and she was so thirsty. The worst part was keeping her eyes open; the lids felt exceptionally heavy and without much effort she could have crawled into bed and slept for a month.

The music stopped and Paul made an announcement that brought instant silence. The villagers shuffled forward and formed a large circle around Paul, Caroline and the priest.

Caroline smiled and momentarily closed her eyes, awaiting the announcement that appeared to be forthcoming. She felt so warm and relaxed. These wonderful, wonderful people were holding some kind of ceremony to welcome her. If only she could stay awake.

Father Nabokov began speaking in what Caroline assumed was Russian, his voice soft and reverent. The smell of incense filled the air. She made an honest effort to listen, but the priest's words were low and monotonous. The others in the room seemed to give heed to his message and Caroline glanced around, smiling now and again.

"Caroline?" Paul's strong voice cut into her musings.

"Hmm." She realized the meeting hall was quiet, each serious brown face regarding her expectantly as though they were waiting for some kind of announcement from her. Paul slipped an arm around her waist, pulling her closer to his side.

"Would you like him to repeat the question?" Paul questioned softly, regarding her with a thoughtful frown.

"Yes, please," Caroline said quietly. If she knew what these people expected of her, then maybe she'd understand. "What's he saying?"

"It's in Russian. He's asking you if you'll cherish and obey me."

Chapter Two

Cherish and obey?'' Caroline repeated, stunned. This welcoming reception was more than she could understand. How she wished she hadn't had quite so much of her aunts' brew. Obviously this little get-together in her honor was some kind of elaborate charade—one in which Caroline had no intention of participating.

The circle of round faces continued to stare anxiously at her, each growing more and more distressed with the amount of time it took for her to respond to the simple question.

''Caroline?'' Even Paul's gruff voice revealed his uneasiness.

Caroline opened her mouth to announce that if they were going to play silly tricks on her, she didn't want to have anything to do with this party. She looked at

Paul and blinked. "I thought you were going to be my guide." Apparently folks took the guiding business seriously in these parts.

Father Nabokov smiled gently. "He will guide you all through your life, child."

A clatter rose from the crowd as several started arguing loudly. Father Nabokov raised his arms above his head and waved in an effort to bring order to the party. "Miss Myers." He paused to wipe his brow with a clean kerchief that magically appeared from inside his huge sleeve. "This is an important decision. Would you like me to repeat the question?"

Paul's intense blue eyes cleared as his gaze pinned hers, demanding that she answer the priest.

An older man, an Athabascan Indian who was apparently a good friend of Paul's, interceded. "You can't back down now—you agreed earlier."

"I did?" What had her aunts gotten her into now? Everyone continued to glare at her and Caroline grew unsettled at the resentment that flared briefly in the brown-eyed stares. "Could I have something cold to drink?"

"It's a bit unusual," Father Nabokov said, clearly discomposed. For a second time, he reached for the kerchief and rubbed it over his brow and one eye.

"Walter," Paul called to the older man who immediately stepped forward.

A minute later, the white-haired Athabascan approached the three with a tall glass of champagne. Paul handed it to Caroline, who hurriedly emptied the contents and sighed audibly as the bubbly liquid tickled the back of her throat. She returned it to the man

Paul called Walter and smiled her thanks. "This is excellent champagne."

Walter nodded abruptly and glanced briefly in Paul's direction. "Paul wanted the best for you."

Caroline noted the censure in the old Indian's voice and again felt a growing sense of unease. "What was it you wanted me to say again?"

Paul's posture stiffened and he expelled an impatient sigh. "Yes would suffice."

"All right then," she agreed in an attempt to be as amicable as possible. Everyone had gone through so much trouble on her behalf, cooking and planning this reception for her arrival. She hated to disappoint them, although she briefly wondered if all tourists were subjected to this type of party—the priest, the incense, the two altar boys robed in white, not to mention the entire village. Her lovely, adorable aunts had sent her to the one place in the world where she would feel welcomed and secure.

"You do?" Father Nabokov looked greatly relieved.

"Sure," she concurred brightly and shrugged her shoulders expressively. "Why not?"

"Indeed." The priest grinned, then grew serious and turned his attention to Paul. The priest's eyes glowed as he gazed upon them both. Caroline felt Paul slide his arm around her once again, but she didn't object. She attempted to give the man of God her full attention, but the room was so warm and everything was so pleasant. She fanned her face with both hands and with some difficulty kept a stiff smile on her lips.

Paul took her right hand and slipped a simple gold band on her ring finger. It looked like a friendship ring and Caroline thought it a fitting gesture. These people did seem friendly.

"I now pronounce you man and wife," Father Nabokov proclaimed solemnly and raised his right hand, moving it in the sign of the cross as he granted them a spiritual blessing. "You may now kiss the bride."

Wife! Kiss the bride! Caroline was completely stunned. She tried to smile, but none would come. She turned to Paul, her eyes filled with questions.

"That's not right, is it?"

Paul didn't answer her. Instead, he turned her in his arms and his gaze narrowed longingly on her face. Before she had the opportunity to voice her uncertainties, Paul lowered his head toward hers. Caroline's heart thundered nervously and she laid her hands on his chest and gazed up at his bearded face. Surely he could tell that she was stunned. A wedding ceremony! She must be dreaming. That was it—this was all part of a dream. Paul's cobalt-blue eyes softened. Gradually, as though in slow motion, his mouth settled warmly over hers. His touch was firm and experienced, moist and gentle—ever so gentle. *Nice dream,* Caroline mused, *very nice, very real.* She hadn't expected a man of his size and vocation to be so infinitely tender.

Enjoy it, girl, Caroline thought, kissing him back with all the eagerness she could muster. Dreams were over far too quickly. The world spun off kilter, so she slipped her arms around Paul's neck to help maintain her balance. Bringing her body closer to his was all the encouragement he needed. His hands slid over her hips, pressing her ripe body invitingly against his own. His grip tightened and molded her torso to his so that her breasts were flattened against his hard chest. Willingly, Caroline surrendered to the sensual upheaval. From the moment Larry had left her at the altar, she'd been dying to be held in a man's arms and kissed as though there was no moment but this one, priceless space in time.

Father Nabokov cleared his throat, but Caroline paid no mind to the priest's appeal. She may have had her doubts about Paul, but she willingly admitted he was one great kisser. Breathless, they broke apart, but continued to stare at each other, lost in the wonder of the overwhelming response.

Paul draped his wrists over Caroline's shoulder. A hint of a cynical smile touched his mouth. "For a minute there I didn't think you were going to go through with it."

"Is this a dream?" Caroline asked.

Paul gave her a funny look. "No."

She laughed. "Of course you'd say that."

His eyes were as blue as anything Caroline had ever seen and she felt lost in the fathomless depths. The tremulous smile she gave him was by a mouth still on fire from his kiss. Involuntarily, she moistened her lips and watched as his gaze darkened.

"Let's get out of here," he growled. Briefly his eyes left hers. Without another word, he hauled Caroline into his arms in one movement and stalked toward the door.

Caroline gasped at the unexpectedness of the action, but the villagers went crazy, resuming the dancing and singing. "Where . . . where are we going?"

"The cabin."

"Oh."

Already his lengthy strides had carried him halfway across the floor. The Athabascans cleared a path and Walter stood ready, grinning almost boyishly as he opened the large wooden doors. Walter chuckled as Paul moved past him. "Don't be so impatient. You've waited this long."

Paul growled something under his breath that Caroline couldn't understand and continued walking.

"How far is the cabin?" she asked dreamily.

"Too far," Paul said with a throaty chuckle. Her ready response to his kiss had been a jolting shock. He'd thought he should progress to their lovemaking with far less urgency—court her, let her become acquainted with him first. Yet the moment her mouth had opened to his, he'd recognized that there wasn't any reason to wait.

Leaning back in his arms, Caroline sighed wistfully. "Why is it dark?"

"It's October, love."

"Love?" she repeated, and sudden tears misted her eyes. She hadn't expected to be anyone's love—not after Larry—not for a very long time.

Paul went still. He could deal with anything but her tears. "What's wrong?"

"Nothing," she murmured, and sniffled. She should know not to drink champagne. Tears had always been a by-product of Dom Perignon.

"I want to know." He smoothed the hair from her temple and softly kissed her there. His words revealed a stark truth: he cared. He was the kind of man who would do all he could to make her world right.

If he hadn't been so tender, so gentle, Caroline could have fought against the unwelcome emotion. But he was all that and so much more. She felt hot tears sear a path down her flushed face and she bit the corner of her bottom lip. "He left me," she whispered through the pain.

"Who?"

"Larry." She turned abruptly, wrapping her arms around Paul's neck, and sobbed into his shoulder. Caroline hadn't believed there were any more tears left in her, but her aunts' tea and the champagne had weakened her resolve to put Larry from her mind.

"You loved him?"

She nodded and sniffled. "Sometimes I wonder if I'll ever stop."

The words stabbed his heart with the brutality of an ice pick. He'd known, or at least he should have known, that a woman like Caroline Myers wouldn't have agreed to marry him and live in the Alaskan wilderness without good cause. Her letter had been so brief, so polite, unlike the others who had tried to impress him with their wit and entice him with the promise of sexual fulfillment.

To his utter amazement, the response to his brief advertisement had been overwhelming. Dozens of letters had poured in that first week, but he hadn't bothered to read any once he'd opened Caroline's. Her picture had stopped him cold. The wheat-blond hair, the incredibly blue eyes that had spoken to him as clearly as the words of her letter. She was honest and forthright, sensual and provocative, mature and trusting. A shining jewel ready to crown a man's life. His life. His jewel. The next day he'd mailed her the airplane ticket and for the past two weeks had waited in eager anticipation for this minute.

"In time, you'll learn not to love Larry," he told her gently, kissing her temple.

With her arms around his neck, Caroline nestled her head against his chest and sniffled again. "I don't know why I told you about Larry. I don't want to think about him anymore. I really don't, but he's there in my thoughts every minute."

"I'll chase him away," Paul teased.

"But how?"

"I'll find a way."

Silently they approached the log cabin and Caroline smiled at how quaint it looked with a huge set of moose antlers above the wooden door. A stepladder was leaning to the right of the only window and a huge woodpile that reached all the way to the eaves was beside that. An oblong, galvanized steel tub hung to the left of the door along with a pair of tightly laced snowshoes.

"It's so homey; you must love it here," Caroline said in awe as she noted the soft light in the lone window.

"I do."

"I'm going to like it." The sigh came all the way from her soul.

Paul paused outside the door and awkwardly bent down to turn the handle. The warmth that greeted them was all the convincing Caroline needed to make this tiny cabin feel like a second home. "I love it," she said, looking around.

Without question, the cabin was small—so compact that the living room and kitchen were compressed into one. Bookcases stood beside a large potbelly stove, and a kitchen counter lined the opposite wall. A doorway led to another room that Caroline assumed was to be her bedroom. Everything was spotlessly clean.

Reluctantly, Paul released her from his arms. Her feet touched the floor and she stepped back. She barely knew the man, yet had spilled her deepest darkest secrets to him as though he were a lifetime friend. "Are . . . are you staying?"

"Would it embarrass you?"

She blinked twice. Once again they were involved in a conversation she didn't quite comprehend. It was the alcohol, Caroline assumed, and shook her head to clear her muddled thoughts. "If you don't mind, I think I'd like to go to bed."

One side of Paul's mouth edged upward. "I was hoping you'd suggest that. Would you feel more comfortable if I left?"

"Perhaps that would be best. I have lots of questions for you, but I'm too sleepy now. We'll talk in the morning. Okay?" She took a step toward the doorway and her peripheral vision picked up the sight of the silky fur-hemmed nightgown that had been a gift from her two aunts. It was spread across the top of the large brass bed, and resembled a lifeless ghost.

"I'll give you some time alone then," Paul said, heading for the front door.

It closed after him and Caroline stood in the middle of the cabin, wondering at the puzzling events of the day. She'd traveled thousands of miles, participated in some strange Alaskan ceremony, thought she was in a dream, kissed a man whose name she barely knew and then wept in his arms. Alaska was some kind of state!

Moving into the single bedroom, undressing as she went, Caroline paused to admire the thick, brightly colored handmade quilt. The small lamp on the table illuminated the room and Caroline recognized her clothes hanging beside those belonging to a man. Probably Paul. He was a gentleman. She didn't know what the craziness was all about; she'd settle that in the morning. She might even be married. A giggle escaped her as she sat on the edge of the mattress. Married! Wouldn't Larry love that. Paul would understand that there'd been a mistake. Her initial impression of him had been wrong; he'd intimidated her at first, but he was actually gentle and caring. She'd witnessed that quality in him a multitude of times in just the past hour.

Her clothes fell onto the floor as she stripped. With complete disregard, she kicked them under the bed. In the morning, she'd remember to pick them up.

The sheer gown slid over her outstretched arms and down her torso. The fur tickled her calves and Caroline smiled, recalling John's comment about the fur keeping her neck warm. It appeared that Alaskan men had a sense of humor, although she hadn't been overly amused at the time. Married! This simply had to be a dream.... When she woke, they'd straighten everything out.

The bed was soft and warm, and Caroline crawled between the sheets, stifling a wide yawn. Her head was cushioned by a thick feather pillow and her last thought before she flipped off the lamp was of the mountain she'd seen from the plane—Denali. Somehow its magnificence comforted her and lured her into a gentle sleep.

Outside, Paul paced the area in front of the cabin, glancing at his watch every twenty seconds. He was cold and impatient now. With the music from the reception echoing around him, he refused to return to the meeting hall. Caroline had wanted some time to prepare herself and he had reluctantly granted her that, but he wasn't pleased. In time she'd learn to be less shy; there wouldn't be room for modesty when winter arrived.

Once he was certain that she'd had as much time as any woman would possibly require, Paul returned to the cabin. The bedroom light was out and he could see the outline of her figure in the bed. His bed. Waiting for him. He recalled the way her soft, lush body had felt against his. With vivid clarity he remembered the way her big blue eyes had looked at him when she had suggested going to bed. Then she'd asked him if she was dreaming. The woman was drunk—drunk on her wedding night. From the time he'd received her letter, Paul had decided to wait for the rewards of marriage until she was ready. But oh Lord, that kiss. For a moment he'd thought she had been as eager as he. He wanted their lovemaking to be slow and easy, but hadn't anticipated her effect on him to be this powerful. The restraint required not to rush to her side weakened him. The taste of her lips lingered on his own and the sample left him craving more. He yearned to hold her breasts and feel their scrumptious weight in his palms. He hungered to taste the sweetness of her mouth again. Pausing to chase away a vision of her, he took a deep breath and leaned against the counter.

In an effort to gain perspective, Paul took down the bottle of Jack Daniel's from the cupboard and poured a stiff drink. He had to think things through. He was convinced she didn't believe their marriage was real, yet she had to know that he had brought her all this way for exactly that purpose. During the wedding she'd looked so confused and unsure. As her husband, he fully expected to claim his marital rights, only he preferred to wait until she was a tad more sober. He wanted a wife and had made that evident in his letter. This was to be a real marriage in every way, and she had come to him on his terms without question. Yet he felt as nervous as a callow youth.

He sat at the table and downed the drink, waiting for its numbing effect. If anything, sitting there and thinking about Caroline in his bed, dressed in that see-through silk gown, had the opposite effect upon him. He'd hoped to cool his passion with sound reasoning and good whiskey, but had ended up fanning the flames.

Standing, Paul delivered the empty glass to the sink and noted that his hands were trembling. He felt like a coiled spring, tense, ready. Oh yes, he was ready.

He moved into the bedroom and undressed in the dark, taking time to fold each piece of clothing and set it on top of the dresser. For a moment he toyed with the idea of sleeping elsewhere, but quickly rejected the thought. He'd be the laughingstock of the entire community if he spent the night anyplace but beside Caroline.

She was asleep, he realized from the evenness of her breathing. Silently he thanked God for that. Five minutes earlier and he would have come to her like a wild beast. As it was he was barely able to restrain himself.

The mattress dipped as he carefully slid in beside her. She sighed once and automatically rolled into his arms, nestling her head against his chest. Paul's eyes widened with the force of his resolve.

Without pause, Caroline stroked her fingertips over his lean ribs. He swallowed convulsively against the sweet torture of her touch and strengthened his self-possession by gently removing her hands from his torso. If only she could appreciate what he was giving up.

"Love," he whispered in her ear, brushing back the thick curtain of blond hair. "Roll onto your side, okay?"

"Hmm?" Caroline was having the sweetest dream. Not for a moment did she believe the man beside her was real. He was part and parcel of the warm, exciting fantasy that had begun earlier.

"I know you would prefer to wait." Paul couldn't believe he was telling her this; she'd come so willingly into his arms.

"Wait?"

"Never mind," he whispered. "Just go back to sleep." Unable to resist, he kissed her gently on the brow and shifted his weight away from her.

Unexpectedly, the comforting, irresistible warmth beside her moved and Caroline edged closer to it. With a sigh of longing, she buried her face in the hollow of his neck.

"Caroline, please, this is difficult enough," he whispered, inhaling harshly. She flattened her hand against his tight abdomen and slowly brushed her lips over his.

With every muscle, Paul struggled for control. Any second and he'd be irrevocably and completely lost. He feasted on her mouth with the intense hunger of a greedy, starving man. Caroline's mouth opened to his as their tongues met, warred, dueled and surrendered. Paul was the one to break the contact, twisting so that he lay on his back. His control was slipping fast; another minute and he wouldn't have been able to stop. Her mouth—oh what a mouth she had, soft and more luscious than any honey he'd ever tasted.

Caroline felt unbearably hot. She loved the secure surroundings; if only she didn't feel like she was sitting on top of a fireplace. The thought was so illogical that she bolted upright, giggled and tossed the blankets aside. She fell back onto the pillow and raised her hands above her head, intertwining her fingers. The ceiling was spinning around and around. In an effort to block out the dizzying sight, she closed her eyes and sought anew the security of the dream resting at her side.

Again Paul tried to move away from her and again had little success. Caroline wanted him close. She couldn't understand why he kept leaving her. If he was part and parcel of her dream, the least he could do was stick around for the fun part. She reached for him again, locking her arms around his neck, kissing him.

"Caroline, for God's sake, stop it."

"Why?"

"Because you're drunk," he hissed.

She giggled. "I know." Her fingers roamed over his sleek shoulders. "Please kiss me again. Has anyone ever told you that you're a great kisser?"

"I can't kiss you." *And remain sane,* he added silently.

"But I want you to." She sounded like a whiny child and the sound shocked her. "Oh, never mind, I wouldn't kiss me either." With that she let out a noisy yawn and pressed her cheek against his hard chest. "You have nice skin," she murmured before closing her eyes.

"You do too," he whispered, and ran his hand down the length of her spine. "Very nice."

"Are you sure you don't want to kiss me?"

Paul groaned. His nobility had some restrictions and he wasn't going to be able to hold off much longer with her wanting him to hold and kiss her every ten seconds.

A soft, purring sound came from deep within her throat as she sighed. He felt like velvet—warm, smooth, and so inviting. Caroline purred again and closed her eyes. It wasn't until later that she realized that the prickly feeling over her soft breasts was caused by his chest hairs. Her hands reveled in his strength as they roamed down the corded muscles of his shoulders.

"Good night, love," he whispered, kissing the crown of her head. He continued to hold her close, almost savoring the sweet torture.

Caroline smiled, content. Just before she gave into the irrepressible urge to sleep, she felt his kiss, and prayed that all her dreams would be this real and this delicious.

Snuggling closer to the warmth at her side, Caroline woke slowly. Her first conscious thought was that her head ached. It more than ached; it throbbed with each pulse and with every sluggish heartbeat as her memory returned, muddled and confused. She rolled onto her back, holding the sides of her head between her hands, and groaned aloud. She was in bed with a man she barely knew. Unfortunately, he appeared to be well acquainted with everything there was to know about her. Extremely well acquainted. Her first inclination was to kick him out of the bed. He'd taken advantage of her inebriated state, and she bit back bitter words as a flush of hot embarrassment brightened her cheeks.

Opening her eyes and looking at him were impossible tasks. She couldn't face the man.

"Good morning," the deep male voice purred.

"It . . . wasn't a dream, was it?" she asked in a tone that was faint and apprehensive.

Paul chuckled. "You mean you honestly don't remember anything?"

"Some." She kept her eyes pinched shut, too mortified to face him.

"Do you remember the part about us getting married?"

Caroline blinked. "I'm not sure."

"In case you don't, I suppose I should introduce myself. I'm Paul Trevor, your husband."

Chapter Three

"Then it was real!" Still holding her head, Caroline struggled to a sitting position. Gradually her eyes opened and she glared down at the bearded man beside her.

Paul was lying on his side, watching her with an amused grin. He leaned on his elbow and slowly shook his head. "I can hardly believe that you didn't expect to be married."

The heat in her face was enough to keep the cabin warm for the entire winter. "I knew at the time you...you weren't all dream." She was honest even at the expense of her stubborn pride.

"We're married, love."

"Stop calling me your love. I am not your or any other man's love, and we've certainly got to do something about annulling this marriage.'' She winced at the flash of pain that shot through her head.

''If you'd rather I didn't call you love, I won't.''

''Call me Caroline or Miss Myers, anything but your love.''

''I am your husband.''

''Will you stop saying that?''

''I have the paperwork to prove it.''

Caroline tucked the blankets under her arms and scowled at him with all the fury she could muster. ''Then I challenge you to produce them.''

''As you wish.'' He tossed aside the blankets and climbed out of the bed, standing only partially clothed before her.

Caroline gasped and looked away. ''I would really appreciate it if you'd put something on.''

''Why?'' He tossed a questioning glance over his shoulder.

The red flush seeped into her ears and she swallowed convulsively. ''Just do it. . . . Please.''

Chuckling, Paul withdrew the slip of paper from his shirt pocket. ''Here,'' he said, handing it to her.

Caroline grabbed it from his fingers and quickly unfolded it. Disregarding the effort it took to read, her gaze quickly scanned the contents. The document looked official enough and her name was signed at the bottom, although she barely recognized the signature as her own. Vaguely she remembered Paul having her sign some papers when they had entered the meeting hall. At the time, Caroline had been so bemused she'd thought it was something to do with registering a guest.

"I signed first," Paul explained, "and gave you the pen."

"Yes, I remember...but at the time I assumed it was something all tourists did." It sounded so ridiculous now that she wanted to weep at her own stupidity. "The party yesterday was our wedding reception, wasn't it?"

"Yes."

Caroline shook her head in utter bewilderment. "I . . . I thought Atta received so few tourists that they greeted everyone like that."

"Caroline, you're not making any sense."

"I'm not!" she shouted, and winced. "You should look at it from my point of view."

"But you agreed to marry me weeks ago."

"I most certainly did not!"

"I have the letter."

"Now that's something I'd like to see. I may not have been in full control of my wits yesterday, but I know for a fact I'd never heard of you until..." The words died on her lips. "My aunts—my romantic, idealistic, scheming aunts...they couldn't have. They wouldn't..."

Paul regarded her suspiciously. "Whose aunts?"

"Mine. Just get the letter and p-please..." she stammered, "please put something on. This is all extremely embarrassing."

Grumbling under his breath, Paul reached for his pants and slipped them over long legs, snapping them at the waist. Next he unfolded his shirt and slipped his arms inside the long sleeves, but he left it unbuttoned. "There. Are you satisfied?"

"Somewhat." Speaking of clothes reminded Caroline of her own state of skimpy dress. When Paul's back was turned, she scooted to the very edge of the mattress in a frantic search for her cords and sweater. She remembered undressing, but she couldn't recall where she'd placed her things.

Stretching as far as possible while in a crouched position, Caroline flung her hand down and made a wide sweep under the bed and managed to retrieve her sweater. Fearing Paul would return at any minute, she slipped her arms into the bulky sleeves and yanked it over her head. Shaking her hair free of the confining collar, Caroline came eye to eye with Paul.

He stood over her, his grin slightly off center. "Just give me that letter," Caroline demanded.

"Would you like me to read it to you?"

"No." She grabbed for it. "I don't appreciate these sophomoric games, Paul Trevor."

"Go ahead and read it for yourself while I fix us something to eat."

"I'm not hungry," she announced sharply, jerking the envelope from his hand. Food was the last thing on her mind at the moment.

Humming as though he hadn't a care in the world, Paul left the bedroom while Caroline's eyes narrowed on his back. The audacity of the man to appear unruffled at this unexpected turn of events was too much for her usually bright sense of humor.

The instant Paul was out of sight, Caroline tore into the letter. The creases were well worn and with a mild attack of guilt she realized that he'd read the neatly typed page repeatedly.

Dear Paul,

My name is Caroline Myers and I'm responding to your advertisement in the Seattle *Post-Intelligencer*. I am seeking a husband to love. My picture is enclosed, but I'm actually more attractive in person. That isn't to say I'm the least bit vain. I enjoy fishing and hiking and Scrabble and other games of skill. Since I am the last of the Ezra Myers family left in the Northwest, I look forward to having children. I'm a nurse currently employed by Dr. Kenneth James, but can leave my employment on two weeks' notice. I look forward to hearing from you.

                                        Most sincerely,

The evenly shaped letters of her name were penned at the bottom of the page in what Caroline recognized as her Aunt Mabel's handwriting.

With sober thoughts, Caroline dressed and joined Paul in the kitchen. He pulled out a chair for her and handed her a cup of coffee.

She laid the letter on the table. "I didn't write this."

"I thought that might have been the case." He wasn't sure of what was happening, but he knew one thing—they were married and he'd waited too long to give her up now.

Her face flushed, she wondered just what *had* happened after the ceremony. Oh Lord, she should remember something as important as that. "I have these two maiden aunts...." Caroline hedged, not knowing where to start an explanation.

"So I gathered." He pulled out the chair across from her and set his elbows on the table. "They answered my advertisement?"

"Advertisement? Apparently so."

"How'd they convince you to marry me?"

"That's just it.... They didn't." Caroline dumped a tablespoon of sugar into the coffee and stirred it several times.

"Then why did you go through with it?"

"I...wasn't myself yesterday. I...I didn't fully realize what was happening." She recognized how utterly ridiculous that sounded, and hurried to explain. "You see, Aunt Mabel and Aunt Ethel—they're actually my great-aunts, but I've always just called them Aunt—anyway, they told me they were giving me a trip to Alaska."

"Why?"

She wasn't sure of how much she wanted to reveal. She understood the reason her two scheming aunts had answered Paul's personal ad. They'd been worried about her after the breakup with Larry. The question was how was she going to untangle herself from this unfortunate set of circumstances. "The purpose for my agreeing to come to Alaska isn't important."

"Few people choose to visit Alaska on the brink of winter."

She wished he would stop arguing with her. Keeping her cool under these conditions was difficult enough.

"Was it because of Larry?"

Caroline felt her blood run cold, then rise to her face. "They told you about Larry?"

"No, you did."

"I did!" Her blue eyes clashed with his and then quickly lowered. "Oh Lord, is there anything I didn't tell you?"

"I imagine there's quite a bit." He paused to drink his coffee. "Please go on. I'm curious about how you got yourself into this predicament."

"Well, Aunt Mabel and Aunt Ethel insisted I take this trip. I'd never been to Alaska and they kept telling me how wonderful the fishing and hiking is. I didn't know how they could afford it, but . . ."

"They didn't."

"What do you mean?" She wrapped her fingers around the hot mug. This was getting more complicated by the minute.

"I paid for it."

"Terrific," she groaned. She'd need to repay him for that and God only knew what else.

"Then John Morrison met me in Fairbanks and the ride to Atta got a bit rugged and in order not to show him how frightened I really was, I drank the thermos of tea my aunts sent along."

"Tea?"

"Not regular tea," Caroline corrected. "My aunts have a special brew—their father passed the recipe on to them."

"I see." One corner of his lip curved upward in a futile effort to contain his smile.

Caroline wasn't fooled. "Damn it, would you stop looking amused? We're in one hell of a mess here."

"We are?" He cocked one eyebrow expressively. "We're married, Caroline, and the ceremony is as legal as it gets. We stood before God and man with the whole village as witness.''

''But you don't honestly expect me to honor those vows.... You can't be that unreasonable.''

''We're married.''

''It was a mistake!''

''Not as far as I'm concerned.''

''I'll have it annulled,'' she threatened.

His grin was wide and cynical. ''After last night?''

Her cheeks flamed even hotter. So something had happened. ''All right,'' she said tightly, ''we'll get a divorce.''

''There will be no divorce.''

''You can't be serious! I have no intention of staying married to you. Good heavens, I don't even know you.''

''You'll have plenty of time for that later.''

''Later? Are you nuts? I'm not staying here a second longer than necessary. There's been a terrible mistake and I want out before something more happens.''

''And I say we make the best of the situation.''

He was being completely unreasonable. ''Just how do you propose we do that?''

''Stay married.''

''You're crazy.'' She stood up so abruptly that the ladder-back chair went crashing to the floor. ''Let's talk this out in a logical fashion.''

''The deed is done.'' As far as Paul was concerned, there was nothing to discuss; she was here in his home and they were legally married. He wasn't going to let her leave him now.

"Deed," Caroline echoed, feeling slightly sick to her stomach. "Then we...I mean last night, you and I...we...?" Her eyes implored him to tell her what had happened.

Paul yearned to assure her that they had shared only a few kisses, but the instant he explained that nothing—well, almost nothing—had happened, she'd bolt. "Caroline, listen to me. It's too late for argument."

"Not from my point of view." Her arms were wrapped around her stomach as she paced the floor. "I want out of here and I want out now."

Paul's mouth thinned with irritation. "That's unfortunate because you're staying."

"You can't force me."

His frustration was quickly mounting. "Would you give us a chance? I'll admit we're getting off to a shaky start, but things will work out."

"Work out!" she cried. "I'm married to a man whose face I can't even see."

Paul ran his hand over the neatly trimmed beard. "It's winter and my beard is part of nature's protection. I won't shave until spring."

"I...I don't know you."

Despite himself, he chuckled. "I wouldn't say that."

"Will you stop bringing up the subject of last night?"

Caroline was surprised by Paul's low chuckle. "Now what's so damn funny?" she demanded.

"You're a passionate woman, Caroline Trevor. If it's this good between us in the beginning, can you imagine how fantastic it will be when we know each other better?"

"Stop it!" Furious, she stalked across the room and stood in front of the small window. A thin layer of snow covered the ground and in the distance Caroline made out the form of a small plane against the blue sky. Her heart rate soared as she contemplated her means of escape. If the plane landed in Atta, she could sneak out before Paul discovered she was missing. Hope sprang eternal.

"Caroline?"

She turned back to him and pressed her hand to her breast. "Were you so desperate for a wife that you had to advertise? That doesn't say a whole lot about your sterling character."

"There are few opportunities in Alaska, love. I don't often get into Fairbanks."

"I already asked you not to call me that."

"I apologize."

He didn't look the least bit contrite and his attitude infuriated her further. "Why did you choose me? You must have received more than one response."

"I received several." *Hundreds, if the truth be known.* "I chose you because I liked your eyes."

"Wonderful!" She tossed her hands in the air.

"But your aunts were right—you are more attractive in person."

Caroline couldn't believe what she was hearing. Paul Trevor honestly expected her to honor her vows and live here on this godforsaken chunk of ice. She was frantic now and growing more desperate by the minute. "I . . . have disgusting habits. Within a week you'll be ready to toss me to the wolves."

"There isn't anything we won't be able to work out."

"Paul, please, look at it from my point of view." Her eyes pleaded with him.

Paul struggled with the effect her baby blues had on him. Refusing her anything was going to be damn difficult, but the matter of their marriage was something on which there was no compromise. "We'll discuss it later," he told her stiffly, and turned away from her. "I've got to get out to the station."

"What station?"

"The pump station by the pipeline."

"John told me something about it." Already her mind was scheming. She'd let him go and pray that the plane circling overhead would land. If it did, then she could convince the pilot to get her out of Atta before Paul even knew she was gone.

"I won't be more than an hour or two."

"All right." She slowly rubbed the palms of her hands together. "And when you get back, I'm certain we'll reach some agreement. It could be that I'll be willing to stay."

Paul eyed her suspiciously, not trusting this sudden change of heart. While he shrugged his arms into his coat, he spoke. "I want your word, Caroline, that you'll remain here in the cabin."

"Here? In this cabin?"

"Your word of honor."

Caroline swallowed uncomfortably; she didn't want to lie. Normally she spoke the truth even to her own detriment. "All right," she muttered, childishly crossing her fingers behind her back. "I'll stay here."

"I have your word?"

"Yes." Without flinching, her eyes met his.

"I won't be long." His hand was on the doorknob.

"Take your time." Already, the plane was landing; she could hear it in the distance. "While you're gone, I'll find my way around the kitchen," she said brightly. "By the time you return, I'll have lunch ready."

Again Paul eyed her doubtfully. She sounded much too eager to have him leave, but he didn't have the time to worry now. Giving her a few hours alone to think matters through was best. She'd given him her word and he was forced into trusting her. Already he was an hour late; Walter had said he would stand in for him, but Paul had refused. The station was his responsibility.

The second the door closed after Paul, Caroline dashed into the bedroom and jerked her clothes off the hangers, stuffing them back inside her suitcase. With a sense of guilt, she left the winter gear that Paul had purchased on her behalf. He'd gone to a great deal of trouble and expense for her, but she couldn't be blamed for that.

A quick check at the door revealed that Paul was nowhere within sight. She breathed a bit easier and cautiously walked out. Although the day was clear, the cold cut straight through her thin jacket.

A couple of Athabascan women passed Caroline and smiled shyly, their eyes bright and curious. She returned their silent greeting and experienced a twinge of remorse at this regrettable subterfuge. If he'd been more reasonable, then she wouldn't have been forced into doing something this drastic.

The plane was taxiing to a stop at the airstrip where she had been delivered less then twenty-four hours before.

Caroline watched from the center of town as the pilot handed down several plywood crates. A few minutes later, he arrived with the dogsleds.

"Hi." She stepped forward, forcing a calm smile.

The tall burly man looked surprised to see her. "Hello."

"I'm Caroline Myers." She extended her hand for him to shake and prayed he didn't detect her nervousness.

"Burt Manners. What can I do for you?"

"I need a ride to Fairbanks," she said quickly. "Is there any way you could fly me there?"

"Sorry, lady, I'm headed in the opposite direction."

"Where?" She'd go anyplace as long as it was away from Atta and Paul.

"Near Circle Hot Springs."

"That's fine. I'll go there first, just so it's understood that you can fly me to Fairbanks afterward."

"Lady, I've already got a full load. Besides, you don't want to travel to Circle Hot Springs. It's no place for a lady this time of year."

"I don't care. Honest."

"There isn't any room." He started to turn away from her.

"There must be some space available; you just unloaded those crates. Please." Caroline hated the way her voice whined, but she was desperate. The sooner she got away, the better.

"Is that the warmest coat you've got?"

He was looking for excuses and Caroline knew it. "No. I've got another coat. Can I come?"

"I don't know...." Still, he hesitated.

"I'll pay you double your normal fee," Caroline entreated, and placed her hand on his forearm. "I'm desperate to get to Fairbanks."

"All right. All right." Burt rubbed the back of his neck and shook his head. "Why do I feel like I'm going to regret this?"

Caroline barely heard him as she made a sharp turn and scurried across the snow toward the cabin. "I'll be right back. Don't leave without me."

She arrived back at the cabin breathless with excitement and relief, and hurried into the bedroom. Taking the coat Paul had purchased for her went against everything she'd ever known, but she would repay him later, she rationalized, once she was safely back in Seattle. To ease her conscience, she quickly scribbled out an IOU note and propped it on top of the kitchen table where he was sure to find it along with a quick apology for the lie. Her suitcase remained just inside the doorway. She reached for it with one hand and her purse with the other.

The dogsleds and the men were waiting for her when she returned and she climbed aboard, feeling jubilant. Getting away from Paul had been so much easier than she'd anticipated. Of course he could follow her, but that was doubtful unless he had a plane, and she didn't see a hangar anywhere.

As Burt had explained, the seating was cramped.

He talked little on the short trip, which suited Caroline just fine. There wasn't a whole lot she had to say herself.

The landing strip at Circle Hot Springs looked even more unreliable than the one at Atta. Caroline felt her stomach pitch wildly when the Cessna's wheels slammed against the frozen ground, but she managed to conceal her alarm.

They were met by a group of four hunters who quickly unloaded the plane, delivering the gear into a huge hunting lodge. When they'd finished, one of the men brought out a bottle of whiskey and passed it around. The largest hunter, the one called Sam, offered the bottle to Caroline.

"No thanks," she said shaking her head. "I prefer to drink mine from a glass." Burt had said that Circle Hot Springs wasn't any place for a lady, but she'd assumed he'd been concerned about the climate.

"Hey guys, we've got a classy dame with us." Sam laughed gruffly and handed her the bottle. "Take a drink," he ordered.

Fear sent chills racing up and down her spine as Caroline frantically looked to Burt. "I said no, thank you."

"Lay off, you guys," Burt called. "She doesn't have to drink if she doesn't want to."

An hour later, Caroline was convinced she'd made a horrible error. The men sat around drinking and telling dirty jokes that were followed with smutty songs and laughter. Their conversation, or at least what she could hear of the coarse language, was filled with innuendos directed toward her. The more she ignored them, the more they seemed to desire her attention.

While the men took a break, Caroline crept close to Burt's side, doing everything possible to remove attention from herself.

"You okay?" Burt asked.

"Fine," she lied. "When do we leave for Fairbanks?"

He gave her an odd look. "Not until tomorrow morning."

"Tomorrow morning? That long?" She gulped. Oh good God, what had she gotten herself into now?

"Hey, lady, you asked for this."

"Right." She'd progressed from the frying pan and had landed directly into the hot coals of the fire. "I'll be ready first thing in the morning." Although it was the middle of the afternoon, the skies were already beginning to darken.

The hunting lodge had a large living room with a mammoth fireplace. The proprietor/guide introduced himself and brought out another bottle of whiskey to welcome his latest tenants. Caroline refused a drink and inquired politely about renting a room for the night.

"Sorry, honey, we're all filled up."

His eyes were twinkling and Caroline didn't believe him.

"You can stay with me," Sam offered.

"No, thanks."

"Such a polite little thing, ain't you?" Sam placed his arm around her shoulders and squeezed hard. The smell of alcohol on his breath nearly bowled her over. "The boys and me came here for some fun and excitement and are real glad you decided to join us."

"I'm just passing through on my way to Fairbanks," she explained lamely, and cast a pleading glance at Burt, but he was talking to another one of the men and didn't notice her. She groaned inwardly when she noted the glass of amber liquid in his hand.

"We came into Circle Hot Springs for a little fun. You knew that when you insisted on flying here, I'll bet." Again he gave her shoulders a rough squeeze.

Caroline thought her vocal cords had frozen with fear. As the evening progressed matters turned from bad to worse. After the men had eaten, they grew louder, and even more boisterous. Burt had started drinking and from the looks he was giving her, Caroline wondered just how much protection he'd be if worst came to worst. From the way he was staring at her, Caroline realized he'd be little help against the burly men.

Sam polished off his glass of whiskey and rubbed the back of his hand across his mouth. "I don't know about the rest of you yahoos," he shouted, attracting the attention of the small party, "but I'm game for a little entertainment."

"What do you have in mind?"

"Burt brought it for us. Ain't that right, little lady?"

Caroline's eyes pleaded with Burt, but he ignored her silent petition. "I...I didn't say anything like that, but...but I think you should know, I'm not much of a singer."

The men broke into boisterous laughter.

"I can dance a little," she offered, desperate to delay any arguments and discover a means of escape. Her heart felt as though it were refusing to cooperate with her lungs. She'd never been so scared in her life.

"Let her dance."

The whiskey bottle was passed from one member of the party to the next while Caroline stood and edged her way toward the front door. If she could break free, she might be able to locate another cabin to spend the night. Someplace warm and safe.

"I'll...need some music." She realized her mistake when two of the men broke into a melody associated with stripteasers.

"Dance," Sam called, clapping his hands.

"Sure." Caroline was close to tears of anger and frustration. Swinging her hands at her sides, she did a shuffle she'd learned in tap dance class in the fifth grade.

The men booed her efforts.

She offered them a feeble smile and stopped. "I guess I'm not much of a dancer, either."

"Try harder," someone shouted, and they all laughed again.

The log door swung open and a cold north wind caused the roaring fire in the mammoth fireplace to flicker. The man's head was covered with a large fur-lined hood. He flipped it back and stared at Caroline, his eyes cutting straight through her.

"Paul!" She'd never been so glad to see anyone in her life. She wanted to weep with relief.

"What's going on here?" he questioned gruffly.

"We're just having a little fun," Burt said, coming to a stand. "Do you know the lady?"

Paul looked directly at Caroline and slowly shook his head. "Nope. I've never seen her before in my life."

Chapter Four

Caroline stared with utter astonishment as Paul took a seat with the other men, removing his parka and idly setting it aside. Someone handed him a drink, which he quickly downed. Not once did he glance in her direction.

"Well," he said after a short moment, "what's stopping you? Dance."

"Dance?" Caroline echoed.

"Dance," all the men shouted simultaneously.

"And no more little girl stuff, either."

Caroline's anger simmered just below the surface. Couldn't Paul see that she was up to her neck in trouble? The least he could do was rescue her. All morning he'd kept insisting he was her husband and nothing she could do would change that. Well, good grief, if she ever needed a husband it was now. Instead, he appeared to find her predicament highly amusing. Well, she'd show him!

Heaving a deep sigh, she resumed her soft-shoe shuffle, swinging her arms at her sides. She really did need the music and if the men weren't going to provide it, she'd make her own. "On the good ship Lollipop..." she bellowed out.

The only one she seemed to amuse was Paul, but his laugh would be better described as a snicker. Although Caroline avoided looking at him, she could feel the heat of his anger. All right, so she'd lied. And so she'd taken the coat. She did intend to pay him for it, plus what he'd spent on the airplane ticket.

The men were booing her efforts again.

"I told you, none of that Shirley Temple stuff," Sam shouted, his voice slurred. "You're supposed to entertain us."

As much as she hated to reveal her fright, Caroline stopped and her gaze silently pleaded with Paul. Again he ignored her.

"Take your clothes off," Sam insisted. "That's what we want."

"Paul?" she whispered, and her voice trembled. "Please." When she saw him clench his fists, she knew she'd won.

"All right, guys," he said, agilely rising to his feet. "The game's over. I'd like you to meet my wife."

"Your wife!" In a rush, Burt Manners jumped from his sitting position. "Hey, buddy, I swear I didn't know."

"Don't worry about it."

"She came to me begging to leave Atta. I told her Circle Hot Springs was no place this time of year for a lady, but she insisted."

Paul's mouth thinned. "I know."

"You need me to fly you back to Atta?" Burt offered eagerly.

"No, thanks, I've got someone waiting."

"You do?" Caroline was so relieved, she felt faint. Another minute of this horrible tension would have been unbearable. The men were looking at her as though she were some terrible cheat who had swindled them out of an evening's fun and games. And from the way Paul kept avoiding eye contact, she wondered what he would do to her once they were alone. She'd gone from the frying pan into the fire and then back to the frying pan again.

Burt stepped outside the hunting lodge with them to unload Caroline's suitcase from his plane. With every step, he continued to apologize to Paul until Caroline wanted to scream. Paul already knew that she'd practically begged the other man to take her away from Atta. He didn't need to hear it over and over again.

"Fact is," Burt said, standing beside his Cessna, looking uneasy, "I didn't know you were married. If I'd had any idea she was your wife, I never would have taken the little lady."

Paul offered no excuse for her behavior. He was so silent and so furious that Caroline expected him to explode any minute. Without a word, he escorted her to the waiting plane and helped her inside. Every movement was that of a perfect gentleman. She didn't need him to shout at her to realize he was enraged, his calm screamed at her far louder than an angry tirade.

Once aboard the plane, Caroline smiled weakly at the pilot and climbed into her seat. No sooner had she buckled her safety belt than the engines roared to life and the Cessna taxied away.

Paul remained rigid for the entire flight. By the time they circled Atta, Caroline was weak with dread. For the last forty minutes, all she had been able to think about was what Paul was going to do to her once they landed. He'd been so gentle the day before, and now...now he looked as though it wouldn't take much for him to strangle her. She'd lied to him, stolen from him and embarrassed him in front of his friends. Maybe he'd be so glad to be rid of her that he'd give her the divorce. Maybe this whole fiasco could be annulled. Oh heavens, why wouldn't he tell her what had happened last night? She rubbed her temples, trying to remember the events following her arrival. She remembered him kissing her and how good it felt, but beyond that her memory was a foggy blur.

When the plane approached the runway, Caroline closed her eyes, preferring not to watch the frozen tundra rising to meet the small aircraft. The Cessna jerked hard once, then again, and for a moment Caroline was certain they were going to crash. A fitting end to her day, she thought gloomily: death. She swallowed down a cry of alarm and looked frantically to Paul, who was seated beside her. His face was void of expression, as though such a bumpy landing was nothing out of the ordinary. When they eased to a stop, Caroline sagged against the back of the seat, weak with relief.

The older Athabascan, Walter, was standing with a team of huskies to meet Paul and Caroline. His age- less eyes hardened when he caught a glimpse of Caro- line, and his angry glare could have split a rock.

"See that Bill has a hot meal and place to spend the night," Paul instructed his friend, apparently refer- ring to the pilot.

"Right away."

Once inside the cabin, Caroline turned her back to the potbellied stove and waited. Paul walked past her and carried her suitcase into the bedroom.

Silently, Caroline removed her parka and hung it beside Paul's. The cabin was warm and cozy, dinner was simmering on top of the stove and the enticing smell was enough to make Caroline feel limp. She hadn't eaten all day.

Still, Paul didn't speak and she waited a minute be- fore she broached a conversation.

"Okay, I'm ready," she said when she couldn't stand it any longer. She stood at attention, her fingers clenched together.

"Ready for what?"

"For whatever it is you're going to do to me."

"I'm not going to do anything."

"Nothing?" Caroline uttered in stunned disbelief.

Paul crossed the tiny kitchen and took down two bowls from the highest cupboard.

"But I lied to you."

His eyes narrowed. "I know."

"And I stole the coat."

He nodded.

"And..." Her voice trembled. "I made a fool out of us both."

Paul lifted the lid to the cast iron kettle, filled each bowl to the top with stew and carried them to the table.

Caroline's fingers gripped the back of the kitchen chair. "You must be furious with me."

"I am."

"Then don't you think you should divorce me? I mean—it's obvious that I'm a terrible person. If I were you, I'd be willing to admit I made a bad choice and go on from there." She eyed him hopefully.

He sat down, neatly unfolded the napkin and laid it across his lap. "There will be no divorce."

"But I don't want to be married, I..."

"The deed is done."

"What deed?" she screamed. If she'd had a wedding night, a *real* wedding night, surely she'd remember it.

"We're married," he stated calmly, reaching for his spoon. "Now sit down and eat."

"No." Stubbornly, she crossed her arms over her chest.

"Fine. Then don't eat."

Caroline eyed the steaming bowl of stew. Her mouth began to water and she angrily jerked out the chair. "All right, I'll eat," she murmured hotly, "but I'm doing it under protest." Eagerly, she dipped her spoon into the thick gravy mixture.

"I can tell," Paul said.

When they'd finished, it was Paul who cleared the table and washed the dishes. Wordlessly, Caroline found a dish towel and dried them, replacing the bowls in the overhead cupboard. Her mind was spinning with possible topics of conversation, all of which led to one central issue: their marriage. She earnestly prayed to find a way of getting him to listen to reason.

An hour after dinner, Paul turned off the lights in the living room and moved into the bedroom. Caroline could either follow him or be left standing alone in the dark.

The instant her gaze fell on the bed, Caroline knew she could delay no longer. "Paul, listen to me—there's been a terrible mistake."

"There was no mistake," he countered, starting to unbutton his shirt.

Briefly, Caroline recalled running her fingers through the tufts of dark chest hair. She felt the blood drain from her face and turned away in an effort not to look at him. If there was anything else to remember, she didn't want to do it now. "The mistake wasn't yours, I'll admit to that. But you must understand that I didn't know anything about the wedding."

"We've already been through this and no amount of talk is going to change what happened. We're married, and that's how we're going to stay, so you'd best accept it."

"But I don't want to be married."

Paul heaved a disgusted sigh. "Would it make any difference if I were your beloved Larry?"

"Yes," she cried, then quickly changed her mind. "No, it wouldn't. Oh hell, I don't know."

"The subject is closed," Paul said forcefully. "We won't discuss it again."

"But we have to."

From behind her, Caroline heard Paul throw back the covers and climb into bed. Slowly, she turned, feeling more unhappy and depressed than at any other time in her life.

"Surely you don't believe I'm going to sleep with you?"

"You're my wife, Caroline."

"But..."

"Why do you insist upon arguing? We're married; you are my wife and you'll sleep in my bed."

"I won't."

"Fine," he grumbled. "Sleep on the floor. When you get cold enough you'll come to bed." With that, he rolled onto his side and turned out the light, leaving Caroline standing in the dark. She remained where she was for a full minute, indecisive, exhausted, bewildered.

"Paul?"

"Hmm."

"If I... If I come to bed, will you promise not to touch me?"

A long moment passed. "After the stunt you pulled today, I doubt that I could."

Caroline supposed she should have been relieved, but she wasn't. Slowly, she undressed and climbed between the clean, crisp sheets. She shivered once and cuddled into a tight ball. As weary as she was, she had expected to fall directly into a deep sleep, but she didn't. In fact, a half hour later, she lay warm, cozy and wide awake.

"Paul?" she whispered.

"What?"

She bit into her bottom lip to hold back the tears. "I'm sorry about today."

"I know."

"Under normal conditions, I would never have done anything so stupid."

"I know that, too."

"Do you know everything?" she flared.

"No."

"I'm glad to hear it."

Another five minutes passed. "Paul?"

"What is it now?"

"Good night."

"Good night, love." She could hear the relief in his voice and her eyes drifted closed.

The next thing Caroline knew, Paul was leaning over her, gently shaking her awake.

"Caroline, it's morning."

Her eyes flew open in alarm and she brushed the thick blond hair from her face. "What time is it?"

"Five o'clock. You'll need to get up and get dressed. There's coffee on the dresser for you."

Maybe he'd relented and had accepted the impossibility of their circumstances. She struggled into a sitting position, her eyes finding his. "Up and dressed? Why?" she asked, hoping he had decided to send her back to Seattle.

"You're coming with me."

"Where?"

"To the pump station."

Her spirits sagged. "But, why? I don't know anything about that...."

"I won't trust you alone again. I don't have any other choice but to bring you with me."

"I'm not going to run away again. I promise."

"You promised before. Now get up and get dressed."

"But, Paul, I won't..."

"I don't have time to argue with you. Either you do as I say or I'll drag you out of bed and take you with me dressed as you are."

Caroline didn't doubt him for a second. "Aye, aye, commander," she said in a crisp, militarylike voice and gave him a mocking salute. Furious, she threw back the sheets and reached for her cords.

Caroline never spent a more boring morning in her life. Paul sat her down in a chair and left her to twiddle her thumbs for what seemed like endless hours. After the first thirty minutes, she toyed with the idea of walking back to the cabin, which she found preferable to sitting in a chair, a punishment more befitting a misbehaving child. However, she quickly discarded that idea. All she needed was to have Paul return to find her gone. If he was furious with her after yesterday, it would be nothing compared to his anger if she pulled the same trick twice. So, although she was bored senseless, Caroline stayed exactly where she was.

Paul returned and she brightened, pleased to have some human contact. But to her dismay, he walked directly past her to another desk and took out a huge ledger, proceeding to record data.

"Paul?"

"Shh."

She pressed her lips together so hard her gums hurt.

He lifted his head when he'd finished and glanced at her expectantly. "You wanted something?"

"I want to go back to the cabin."

"No."

"After what happened yesterday, you can't believe I'll try to get away again." He returned to his work and refused to look at her, ostensibly studying his ledger. Caroline's blood was close to the boiling point. "What are you going to do? Keep me with you twenty-four hours a day?"

"You gave me no option."

"You can't be serious. I'm not going to run away." She pointed to the front door. "There are crazy people out there."

He didn't respond.

"Paul, please, I'll go nuts sitting here with nothing to do."

"Get a book and read." His response was as uncaring as the arctic wind that howled outside the door.

"Oh, I get it," she said in a high-pitched, emotional voice. "So this is to be my punishment. Not only are you going to keep me as your prisoner, but I'm to suffer your company as well. How long?"

"How long what?" With deliberate care, he set his pen aside.

"How long before you learn to trust me? A week? Ten days? A month?"

"I can't answer that. It depends on you."

She flew to her feet, her fists knotted. "Well, you'd be wise to never leave me alone again, because the minute I get the chance, I'm high-tailing it out of here. Somehow, some way, I'll find a way to escape. You can't keep a person against his will. This is the United States of America and slavery was outlawed a hundred years ago."

"A hundred and twenty."

"Furthermore, you're the worst possible husband a woman could ever have. I refuse to be your wife no matter what some piece of paper says." She waited for him to argue with her and when he didn't, she continued her tirade. "Not only that... You've got to be the most stubborn man I've ever met. Stubborn and unreasonable and ... and ... chauvinistic to boot!"

Paul nodded. "I know. But given time, you'll learn to love me."

"Never." Caroline vowed. "Not while I breathe."

"We'll see."

He sounded so damn sure of himself, so confident, that she longed to throttle him. Drained, Caroline sank back into her chair. To her horror, tears filled her eyes and fell hot against her cheek. She wiped them aside and sniffled loudly to hold back the flood that lay just beneath the surface. "Paul," she cried softly. "I want to go home. Please."

His mouth grew hard and inflexible. "You are home. The sooner you accept that the better it will be for us both."

With that, Caroline buried her face in her hands and wept until there were no tears left. Her eyes burned and her throat ached.

Paul felt the weight of Denali pressing against his back. Dear God, he prayed he was doing the right thing. He could deal with her harangues, even her feisty anger, but her tears were another matter. They brought all his doubts to the surface. A month—he had promised himself a month. If things weren't better by the end of October, he'd send her back to Seattle. Looking at her now, bent over, weeping as though she hadn't a friend in the world, he felt an overwhelming compassion build up in his heart. It would be so easy to love her. She had spunk and character and was more woman than he had ever dreamed he would find.

By midafternoon, Caroline had read one adventure novel, written her two maiden aunts a scathing letter, destroyed that, and had drawn several pictures of a distorted Paul with a knife through his heart. She couldn't help it; after eight hours of complete monotony, she felt murderous.

Toward evening, Paul handed her her parka. "Are you ready to go back to the cabin?"

Was she ever! But she'd be damned before she'd let him know that. With a regal tilt of her chin, she reached for her jacket and slipped her arms inside the warm, thick sleeves. She hadn't spoken a word to Paul in hours and he hadn't the decency to reveal the least bit of concern. Well, she could hold out longer than he could. By the time she returned to Seattle, he'd be so glad to be rid of her, he'd give her the divorce without so much as an argument.

A thick layer of snow had fallen during the day, and although the cabin was only a short distance from the pumping station, they needed snowshoes to trek their way back. It was the first time that Caroline had ever worn them, and she was forced to squelch her natural delight.

Again, dinner had been left on the stove. Tonight it was a roast with onions, potatoes and carrots simmered in the juice. Caroline wondered who did the cooking, but she refused to ask Paul a thing.

As he had the night before, Paul placed the silverware on the table and delivered their meal from the stove. A couple of times Caroline felt his gaze on her, but she was determined to swallow her tongue before she'd utter a word.

"I must admit," Paul said, halfway through their dinner, "that I prefer the silence to your constant badgering."

"Badgering!" Caroline exploded. "I do not badger. All I want is out of this despicable marriage."

Paul grinned boyishly. "Has anyone told you how expressive your eyes are?"

Caroline pressed her lips together and stabbed her meat with unnecessary force. "I wish that was your heart. Oops, my mistake. You don't have one."

Paul laughed outright at that. "But I do, love," he said gently a few minutes later. "And it belongs to you."

"I don't want it," she cried, struggling to hold back tears of frustration. "Didn't you say you'd received lots of letters in response to your ad for a mail-order bride? Those women all *wanted* to be your wife. Let me go, Paul. Please let me go. I'll repay you the money you've already spent. I swear I will, and I'll..."

"Enough!" He slammed his fist against the table with such force that her water glass toppled. "I'm sick of your pleading. For the last and final time, we're married and we're going to stay married. I refuse to discuss the matter again."

"Yes, your Majesty," Caroline returned, just barely managing to regain her composure.

Neither one of them ate much after that. Caroline toyed with the food on her plate, but her appetite had vanished, and with it her will to fight.

Standing, she carried her plate over to the sink and scraped it clean. Paul brought over his dishes and they worked together silently, cleaning away the dinner mess.

"Paul," she said, after he'd wiped the last dish dry, "do you play Scrabble?" Her question was asked with a hint of practiced indifference. He must; she'd seen the game on his shelf.

"A bit. Why?"

"Could you and I play? Just to help pass the evening."

"I suppose."

For the first time in two days, Caroline's smile came all the way from her heart. Her two aunts loved Scrabble and had taught it to her as a child. With such expert tutoring, she was practically unbeatable. Her whole world turned brighter. "It would be far more interesting, though," she added with a feigned thoughtful look, "if we played for something, don't you think?"

"How do you mean?"

She brought the game down from the shelf and unfolded the board. "Simple. If I win I am granted one request from you and vice versa."

"And naturally you'd ask for a divorce. No way, love."

"No, not a divorce." She would work up to that.

"If not the divorce, what would you request?"

"Privacy."

"Privacy?"

"Yes, I want to sleep alone."

Skeptical, he eyed the recliner. "For how long?"

She'd go easy on him. "One night."

"Agreed." He pulled up a chair, twisted it around and straddled it. "And on the off chance I win?" He could see the mischief in her brilliant blue eyes. She clearly expected to beat him.

"Yes?" She regarded him expectantly. "What would you want?"

"A kiss."

"A kiss?"

"And not a peck on the cheek either. I want you to kiss me so good it'll turn my insides out." With her sweet mouth, that wouldn't take much, he mused.

Caroline hesitated. "But nothing more than a kiss, right?"

"Nothing more. Agreed?"

With a saucy grin, she stuck out her hand. "Agreed." They shook on it and Caroline laughed. It felt so good to laugh again; she hated the constant bickering. Besides, this was going to be like taking candy from a baby.

"Let the games begin," Paul said, grinning back at her.

For a moment, it was hard to take her gaze off him. His eyes were smiling and although she couldn't see his face through the beard, she felt he must be a handsome man. His eyes certainly were appealing. Playfully, she held up her hand and flexed her ten fingers.

"You draw first." In gentlemanly fashion, Paul handed her the small velvet bag with the mixed letters of the alphabet.

Caroline inserted her hand and drew out an A. She gave him a triumphant look and set it on her letter holder. "I go first."

"Right."

It wasn't until they were a couple of plays into the game that Caroline recognized Paul's skill. He was going to give her some stiff competition. In fact, their scores remained close throughout the match. Caroline was down to her last five letters when Paul gained a triple word slot, added up his score and beamed her a proud look.

"Paul!" Caroline glanced at the board and gasped, unable to hold back her shock. "That's a four-letter word! A dirty four-letter word!"

"I'm well aware of that, love."

"You can't use that. It . . . it's indecent."

"It's also in the dictionary. Would you care to challenge me?"

She knew if she did, she would immediately forfeit the game. "No," she grumbled. "But I consider that word in poor taste."

Paul's response was a soft chuckle. "You can challenge me if you wish."

"What's the score?" Five letters left... If she could use them all she might be able to pull into the lead.

"Three hundred and twenty to two eighty-eight," Paul informed her gleefully. "Do you concede?"

"Never!"

"I'm afraid you must. I'm out of letters."

"You won," Caroline said, almost in a daze. She had lost only one game of Scrabble since her junior year in high school. She had played brilliantly, yet Paul had outdone her.

"Yes, love, I won."

Caroline was so stunned that for a minute all she could do was stare at the board in shocked disbelief.

"Love? I believe you owe me a kiss."

She should object to his calling her "love," but she was too bemused to voice her disapproval. "You beat me in Scrabble," she said. "And I'm a good player. Very good."

"I'm fairly well versed at the game myself," Paul added. "There's not much else for Walter and me to do on those long winter nights."

Caroline's eyes narrowed. He'd hustled her into this match, knowing full well that he had a good chance of winning.

"I believe you owe me a kiss," he repeated.

"You cheated," Caroline cried. "You used a four-letter word and..."

"Don't tell me you're a poor sport, too."

As fast as she could, Caroline removed the wooden pieces from the playing board. "You mean in addition to being a liar and a thief."

"I didn't mean it like that," Paul said soberly.

"Well, you needn't worry, I'll give you what I promised, but I still think it's unfair that you used that despicable word."

"You'd use it too," Paul said, folding up the game and placing it back on the bookcase.

"I wouldn't!"

"If you were down to four letters and that word placed you on a triple word score and it would guarantee you a win, then I don't doubt you'd use it!"

"Well," Caroline hedged, a smile lifting the edges of her mouth. "I'd be tempted, but I don't know that I'd stoop that low."

"Yes, you would. Now own up, love."

Reluctantly, Caroline stood and rounded the table to his side.

"A kiss that will turn my insides out," he reminded her.

"I remember," she said ruefully. She stood in front of him and Paul's arm circled her waist, pulling her down onto his lap. She offered him a weak smile and gently placed her hands on his shoulders. His palms slid around her back, directing her actions.

She twisted her head to the right, then changed her mind and moved it left. Slowly, she bent forward and placed her parted mouth over his. His lips were moist and warm and moved lightly, brushing over hers in a slow, sensuous attack. Playfully, Caroline darted her tongue in and out of his mouth, then moved more deliberately until she felt him melt in her arms. His tongue skimmed the inner lining of her mouth as he took command. He kissed her with a wildness that was so much a part of this untamed land. Erotically, he moved his head from side to side, his tongue probing, searching, until she gave him what he wanted—what she wanted.

They broke apart, panting and weak.

"Oh Caroline," he breathed against her neck. Their mouths fused again. Although she'd initially had no intention of giving him more than the one kiss he'd bargained for, she was as eager for the second as he.

Again his mouth nuzzled her neck. "Another game, love? Only this time the stakes will be slightly different."

Chapter Five

Another game of Scrabble?'' Caroline repeated, feeling utterly content.

Dream or not, her memory served her true; Paul Trevor was one fantastic kisser. Caroline's eyes flew open and she jerked herself free from Paul's arms. Mere hours before she'd vowed to freeze him out and here she was sitting on his lap with her arms around his neck, kissing him with all the fervor in her young heart.

"Our Scrabble days are over, Paul Trevor," she said hotly, placing her hand against the table to help maintain her balance. She brushed the hair from her temple and felt a heated flush in her cheeks.

"You mean you're quitting because I'm a better player than you?" Paul returned with a low chuckle.

"Better player, my foot!"

The whole affair appeared to amuse him, which only served to further anger Caroline. She stormed into the bedroom and sat on the end of the bed, sulking. Until she'd met Paul, she'd considered herself an easygoing, fun-loving person. In two days' time he'd managed to change all that. With her arms crossed, she fumed, contemplating a hundred means of making him suffer.

It wasn't until they were in bed, Paul sleeping at her side, that Caroline acknowledged the truth: she was more furious with herself than Paul. He'd played an honorable Scrabble game, except for that one four-letter word, and had won their wager fair and square. What infuriated her most was her overwhelming response to his kiss. She didn't want him to be tender or gentle; it was far too difficult to hate him when he was so caring and so loving.

In the morning, Paul woke her. "Time to get up, sleepyhead," he whispered softly in her ear.

Caroline's eyes fluttered open. Paul sat on the edge of the mattress, smiling down on her. "Coffee's ready," he told her.

"Paul," she pleaded, using her blue eyes to appeal to his better nature. "Do I have to go to the pumping station with you again? It's so boring. I hate it."

"I'm sorry, love."

"I promise I won't pull any tricks. On my mother's grave, I vow I won't do..."

His gaze grew cold and he stood. "No, Caroline, you're coming with me."

Arguing would do no good, she realized with a frown, and dutifully tossed aside the heavy quilts to climb out of bed, grumbling as she did so. Paul left her to dress on her own, and she was grateful for the privacy. God knew there was little enough in this tiny cabin.

Caroline prepared herself for the long, tedious hours. She took with her a deck of cards, some reading material, and a pen and paper.

As he had the day before, Paul joined her at the desk beside her own a couple of hours into the morning. He offered her a gentle smile and pulled out the ledger.

She waited to be certain she wasn't disturbing him before speaking. "Paul, who does the cooking for you?"

He didn't look up from the ledger as he spoke. "Tanana Eagleclaw; you met her the day of your arrival."

"There were so many," she explained feebly.

He grinned, but didn't tease her about her memory lapse.

"Paul," she tried again. "I'm a good cook." That may have been a bit of an exaggeration, she added silently, but anything was better than sitting around this infernal pumping station ten hours every day.

"Hmm." He barely acknowledged her, finding his ledgers more compelling.

"Really, if you must know, I'm an excellent cook." She was getting desperate now. "I could prepare our meals. In fact, I'd like to do it."

"Tanana does an adequate job."

"But I want to do it!"

"You can't."

"Why the hell not?"

"Because you're here with me, that's why not."

"Do you mean to tell me that you're going to drag me here with you for the rest of my life?"

Paul sighed expressively. "We're going over the same territory as yesterday. You'll stay with me until I feel I can trust you again."

"Wonderful." He might begin to trust her sometime close to the millennium. A lot of good that did her now.

A week passed and each morning a sleepy Caroline traipsed behind Paul to the pumping station and each night she followed him home. She hated it and Paul knew it, but no amount of pleading could get him to change his mind. He wanted her where he could see her every minute of every day.

The mail was delivered twice a week and a letter was sitting on the table addressed to Mr. and Mrs. Paul Trevor when they arrived back from the station during Caroline's second week in Atta.

"A letter!" Caroline cried, as excited as a child on Christmas morning. Contact with the outside world. A tie with the past. She hurriedly read the return address. "It's from my aunts."

Paul's smile was gentle. "The two schemers?"

Eagerly, Caroline tore open the envelope. "The very ones." She hadn't quite forgiven them for their underhanded methods of getting her to Alaska, but she missed them dreadfully.

"What do they have to say?" Paul coaxed, watching the smile work across her face as her eyes wove their way over the page.

"They asked me how I like my surprise. In case you don't know, that was you."

"And?" he prodded with a soft chuckle.

"And what?"

"How do you like me?"

It was Caroline's turn to laugh. "I find you... surprising."

"Typical."

"Aunt Mabel, she's the romantic one, says she feels in her heart that we're going to be happy and have... oh my goodness."

"What?"

Color seeped up from Caroline's neck and flushed her cheeks. "She predicts twelve children, which is how many my great-great-grandmother had as a mail-order bride."

"I'm willing," Paul informed her with a toothy grin.

"Be quiet, I'm reading. And Aunt Ethel..." She hesitated, her eyes scanning the remainder of the page. "It was nothing." With her heart pounding frantically, and hoping to appear nonchalant, she refolded the letter and placed it back inside the envelope.

Paul joined her at the kitchen table. "What did she say?"

Caroline dropped her gaze. "It wasn't important."

"Shall I read the letter myself?"

"No..." she said, and hid it behind her back. He could easily have forced her to hand it over, but didn't, although his cutting gaze reminded her that the letter had been addressed to them both and he had every right to read it. "She told me that Larry Atkins unexpectedly dropped by when . . . when he couldn't get ahold of me. Aunt Ethel said she took great delight in telling him I was a married woman now."

"I see," Paul said thoughtfully.

"I'm sure you don't." Caroline braced her hands against the kitchen counter as she battled down a bout of self-pity. Her relationship with Larry had been over weeks before she had come to Alaska. It shouldn't hurt this much now, but it did. Her heart yearned to know why he'd contacted her and how he'd reacted to the news that she was married to Paul. She yearned to let Larry know that it wasn't a real marriage—not the way theirs would have been.

Gently, Paul placed his hands on the rounded curve of her shoulders. "Caroline, here." He turned her into his arms and held her quietly. It wasn't the embrace of a lover, but that of a caring, loyal friend.

She pressed her face against his chest and drew in a wobbly breath. His hand was in her hair, cradling the back of her head as he rubbed his jaw across her crown in a soothing, comforting motion.

"Do you still love him?" he asked after a moment.

Caroline had to analyze her feelings. She'd been crazy in love with Larry for months. They had taken delight in being so different from each other. She missed him, thought about him, wished good things for him. But did she love him?

Paul decided that holding Caroline was like sampling a taste of ambrosia. He'd barely touched her in

a week, wanting to give her time to know him. He
yearned to woo her, to court her. Their relationship
was in an awkward stage; he wasn't convinced he
could trust her yet. From her own mouth he'd been
informed that the first time he left her alone, she'd run
away, and with winter coming on, he couldn't leave
her until he was certain she wouldn't try to escape. He
yearned to hold her and kiss her until he felt he'd go
mad. His successful restraint was sure to make him a
candidate for sainthood. He regretted that he hadn't
made love to her on their wedding night.

From her ramblings that night, Paul knew about
Larry. The situation was far less than ideal and he'd
played the role of the patient husband to his own
detriment. She'd been with him nine days, and yet it
had aged him a hundred lifetimes to have her softness
pressed against him, knowing her thoughts were on
another man.

"Caroline," he pressed, needing to know. "Do you
still love him?"

"I . . . yes," she answered truthfully, her voice
strained and low. This was difficult. Paul was her
husband, in fact if not in deed, although that remained questionable; and she had no desire to be cruel
to him. "You don't stop loving someone because
they've hurt you," she told him softly, relishing the
comfort of his arm. "I'm trying not to love him. . . .
Does that help?"

Tenderly, Paul kissed the side of her face. "It makes
it easier to accept. I appreciate what it cost you to be
honest."

A polite knock at the door drew them apart reluctantly. A shy and very pregnant Indian girl walked in. Her face was dark and round and when her deep, rich eyes fell on Caroline, her smile was almost bashful, as though she felt she had intruded on their lovemaking. "You sent for me, Mr. Trevor?"

"Yes." Paul slipped his arm around Caroline's waist. "Caroline this is Tanana Eagleclaw. Tanana, my wife, Caroline."

"How do you do, Mrs. Trevor?" the girl said formally, dropping her gaze.

"Fine, thank you, Tanana. When is your baby due?" From the looks of her, it could have been any day.

"Six weeks." Again the Indian girl smiled shyly, obviously pleased with the pregnancy.

Caroline guessed that she couldn't be any more than eighteen. "You're a good cook."

"Thank you."

Paul said something to her in her native tongue and the girl nodded eagerly, her gaze briefly moving to Caroline. She left soon afterward.

"What was that all about?" Caroline asked.

"You said you wanted to meet the girl, so I had her come over."

"But that wasn't the only reason. What did you say to her?"

"When?"

"Just now." Caroline gave him a bewildered look until she realized he had purposely played dumb. "Never mind. You obviously don't want me to know, so forget it." She did understand one thing; Tanana's feelings would be hurt if Caroline were to take over the cooking. Perhaps when her baby was born, Caroline could assume the task without there being any loss of pride.

That night, sitting in front of the fireplace, Caroline wrote her aunts a long reply. She told them that in the beginning she was furious over what they'd done, but gradually she'd changed her mind. Paul was a good man, a decent man, and they had chosen well. There was no need to disillusion the two romantics with the truth. She couldn't tell them that she hoped and prayed that, given time, Paul would see fit to let her return to Seattle. That kind of information would only cause the pair to fret. Nor did she tell them that if she was going to be a bride, she wanted the opportunity to choose her *own* husband. When Paul sent her back, and Caroline believed he would, then there would be time enough to explain everything. For now, she would play their game and let them think they'd outsmarted her and that she was a happy, blushing bride. It could do no harm.

That night, Caroline fell into bed, exhausted. Paul joined her soon afterward and as she did each night, she pretended to be asleep when he slipped his body beside her own.

"'Night, love," he whispered gently.

She didn't respond and a few minutes later drifted into a natural, contented sleep.

A noise woke her up and she stirred, chagrined to note that she was sleeping with her head on Paul's hard chest. His arm secured her to him.

"Is it morning yet?" she murmured, closing her eyes again, reluctant to leave the warmth pressing against her.

"In a few minutes."

Paul rose before her every morning to stoke the fire and put on the coffee. Caroline had no idea if she touched him in her sleep and feared that she would wake one morning in his arms and embarrass them both.

"Do I do this often?" she asked, only a little flustered.

"Not near enough," he returned. His hand ran down the length of her spine, stopping at the small of her back as though it was torture to do so. He paused and inhaled sharply.

Caroline realized it was that soft rumble from his throat that had awakened her. The knowledge produced a lazy smile. Still she didn't move. He felt incredibly good—warm, strong...male.

Five minutes passed, then ten. Caroline knew she had to pull herself away; each minute was more pleasant than the one before.

"I'll make the coffee this morning," she murmured, easing her torso from his.

Paul stopped her. "There's no rush. Go back to sleep if you like."

"To sleep?" She lifted her head enough to search his face. "Aren't you going to the station?"

"I'll be there, but you won't."

Caroline was sure she'd misunderstood him.

"I asked Tanana to spend the day with you," he explained. "She's going to introduce you to the other women in the village and show you the ropes."

For a moment, Caroline was too stunned to realize what he was saying. "Paul, oh Paul, do you mean I don't have to go to the station?" Without thought, she wrapped her arms around his neck and, laughing, dropped her mouth over his, covering what she could of his bearded face with a series of tiny, eager kisses.

Paul's hands found her head and guided her mouth to his for a kiss that was long and hard. Leisurely, their lips moved against each other's. Without her being certain how it happened, Paul reversed their positions with such ease that she lay on her back, staring up at him. Their eyes met in the dark, and slowly, as though he couldn't resist her a minute longer, he lowered his mouth to capture hers in a kiss that stirred her heart and her soul. Caroline couldn't have denied herself that kiss to save her soul. Her hands sought the side of his face, luxuriating in the feel of his beard.

Paul broke off the kiss and, with a sigh that came all the way from the marrow of his bones, buried his face in the hollow of her throat.

Caroline entwined her arms around his neck and released her own sigh of contentment. She was shocked at how right it felt to have Paul hold and kiss her. Her heart raged to a pagan beat and her body throbbed with a simmering passion. She didn't want to feel these things. When she left him, she didn't want to be weighted down with regrets.

He raised his head then, and compelled her gaze to meet his own, but she turned her head away. "You're going to be late."

"Right."

No time clock waited for him, and they both knew it. He eased his weight from her and sat on the edge of the bed a moment to gain his strength. Caroline made him weak in ways he didn't fully understand. By rights he should have taken her. She wanted him; he could almost taste her eagerness.

Exasperated, he plowed his fingers through his hair. He'd be patient a little longer, but he wasn't going to be able to withstand many more of her kisses. She drugged him. Fascinated him. Captured his heart and held it in the palm of her hand with as much concern as she would an unwanted sweet.

Although it was midmorning, Caroline was barely up and dressed when Tanana arrived. Again the Indian woman knocked politely at the door before stepping inside.

"Morning, Mrs. Trevor," she said shyly.

"Morning, Tanana. I was just fixing myself some breakfast. Would you like something?"

The Indian woman shook her head. "You come now, please?"

"Now?"

Again Tanana grinned and nodded.

"There isn't time for breakfast?"

"No time."

Muttering disparaging words under her breath, Caroline removed the skillet from the stove and placed the eggs back inside the refrigerator while Tanana grabbed Caroline's fur-lined boots and parka.

"Where are we going?"

"To meeting hall."

"The other women are already there?"

"Many wait."

Caroline hadn't a clue as to what they were waiting for, but she was so pleased to be able to talk to another human being that she wouldn't have cared if they were only going to sit around and drink weak coffee.

As Tanana had promised, there were several women gathered inside the large hall that served as the heart of the small community. Smiling, round faces greeted her when they walked into the room and Tanana led an astonished Caroline to an empty chair that stood in the center of the room—obviously the seat of honor.

She soon recognized that the women were giving a small party in her honor, something like a bridal shower. One by one, each woman stepped forward and offered her a gift. Only some of the women spoke English, but Tanana acted as translator. The gifts were mostly homemade, displaying such talent and skill that Caroline's breath caught in her throat at their beauty. She received a thick hand-knit sweater, slippers made from sealskin, several pieces of intricate scrimshaw with scenes that depicted Indian life in the frozen North, as well as smoked salmon, deer, moose and elk meat. Caroline watched in wide-eyed wonder as they each came to her. They had so little and she had so much, yet they were lovingly sharing a precious part of their lives. A tear gathered in her eye and she swallowed down a thickness forming in her throat, not wanting them to see how much their kindness had affected her.

When they'd finished, Caroline stood and went to each one to personally thank her. Later, after they had served lunch, the women gathered their yarn together and started to work.

"What are they making?" Caroline asked Tanana.

"Sweaters for the tourists."

"Atta gets that many tourists?"

The Indian girl cupped her hand over her mouth and laughed. "No, the stores in Fairbanks, Juneau and Anchorage sell them."

"Oh." Caroline felt like an idiot.

"All the women of the village work on the sweaters in wintertime," Tanana continued. "Each day we gather in meeting hall."

"I knit," Caroline said, broaching the subject carefully. She wanted to be a part of this community. Although her skill might not have been at the level of these women, she could learn. They'd been so kind to her that she wished to return some of their thoughtfulness.

"Would you like to join us?" Tanana asked politely.

"Please." Almost before Caroline knew what was happening, she was handed a pair of needles, several skeins of thick yarn, and with Tanana to guide her, was set to work.

That night, Caroline was bursting with excitement. So much so that she could barely contain it. By the time Paul walked in the cabin door, she practically flew across the room.

"Hi," she greeted, her voice excited. It required a great effort for her to contain her joy and enthusiasm. "Did you know about the...party?"

His smiling eyes delved into hers. "Tanana told me about it last week. She said that it was time I let you out of bed long enough to meet the village women."

Caroline decided to ignore the comment. "They're wonderful people."

"I know, love." He had removed his parka and hung it in the closet when Caroline grabbed his hand and led him into the bedroom. She'd placed the non-food items on top of the quilt for him to examine. He picked up each piece and nodded his pleasure at the village's generosity. When he came to the oddly shaped piece of knitting, he regarded it skeptically. "And what's this?"

"Oh, yes, I nearly forgot. The women knit, but I guess you already know that. Well, anyway, they let me sit and work with them this afternoon. Of course I'm not nearly as good as they and my poor sweater wouldn't be anywhere near good enough to sell to the tourists. We laughed about that. It's amusing that some tourist would buy a sweater they assumed was knit by an authentic Indian only to discover it was crafted by a Seattle nurse." She giggled at the memory. "At the end of the afternoon, I think Tanana was afraid of hurting my feelings so I asked if I could do something else with this first effort."

"And what was that?"

"I told them I wanted to knit this sweater for you."

"What did they say to that?"

"Oh, they were pleased, but then they would be, since they probably couldn't sell it." She waltzed out of the bedroom and into the kitchen. "And I made dinner. Tanana looked so tired that I offered. Naturally, she argued with me, but not too strenuously."

"So you had a good day."

"I had a marvelous day!" She turned her back to him to stir the simmering gravy. All day she'd been trying to come up with a way of approaching Paul about joining the women on a daily basis. He'd been so unyielding in other matters that she dreaded a confrontation now.

"I suppose you want to go back?"

Caroline whirled around, her heart in her eyes. "Can I?"

"I think that's more your decision than mine."

She understood what he was saying, but swallowed down a ready reply while she took the thick slices of meat from the oven and placed them on the table.

"Unless you trust me again," she said softly, her eyes holding his, "I know I won't ever be able to prove that I'm trustworthy."

"Then do as you wish."

Caroline was so pleased that she was hard-pressed not to throw her arms around his neck and kiss him the way she had that morning. It wasn't until after they'd eaten that she realized how much she actually wanted to kiss him, and quickly pushed the thought from her mind.

Later, she found herself humming while washing the dinner dishes, and paused, surprised with herself. She was happy—truly happy and content. She turned to find Paul watching her and they shared a smile.

Once again they played a heated game of Scrabble, but without any wagers. To her delight and disgust, Caroline won.

"You'll note that I didn't use a single dirty word," she told him with a proud snicker.

Paul chuckled and reset the board for a second game.

That next afternoon and for several more that followed, Caroline joined the Indian women for their daily knitting session. The first few days, the women were shy and didn't say much to her. Gradually they opened up and she was privilege to the village gossip. More than one of the women seemed to find something about Caroline highly amusing. Every time they looked in her direction, they leaned over to the woman next to them and whispered something that the other found comical. Finally, when Caroline's curiosity got the better of her, she asked Tanana about it.

The Indian girl blushed. "They say you are fortunate woman."

"Fortunate? I don't understand."

"Yes, you have Paul for your lover. They are envious that at night he sleeps at your side and holds you in his arms. They say you will have many healthy babies with Paul. He is . . . I don't know English word."

"Never mind," Caroline returned, her fingers tightening around the knitting needles. "I know what you mean." Did she ever! So Paul was a virile male who had sampled the delights of the village women before her arrival.

By the time she arrived back at the cabin, Caroline was so furious that she paced the small enclosure, ready to give her husband a solid piece of her mind the instant he returned home. She'd never dreamed, hadn't thought he'd ever do anything that low. No wonder he wanted a wife. From the looks the Indian women had been sending her way, the Athabascans had probably started fighting over him. Well, they could have him. She was finished with him, through. Nothing could keep her in Atta now. She didn't care what it took, she was leaving Paul and the sooner the better.

When the wooden door opened and the howling wind whirled around the enclosed cabin, it was only a spring breeze compared to the ice caking Caroline's heart.

"Hi," Paul greeted her with a ready grin, but one look at her contorted, angry features and his smile quickly faded. "What's wrong?"

She didn't wait for him to remove his coat. Her index finger found its mark in the middle of his chest. "You are despicable. You are lower than a snake. You are..." Words failed her as hot tears blurred her vision. "I can't find the words to tell you how much I despise you!"

Paul didn't look particularly concerned. "Was it something I said, or are you still mad about that four-letter word I used in the Scrabble game?"

Chapter Six

You think you're so clever, don't you?'' Caroline flared. Her outrage got the better of her and she picked up a book from the end table and hurled it at him.

With a dexterity few could manage, Paul caught the book and the saltshaker that immediately followed. The amusement drained from his eyes. ''Caroline, what's gotten into you?''

''You...animal!''

''For God's sake, tell me what I did.''

''You...*beast*!'' The pepper shaker whizzed past his ear.

''Caroline!''

''You...you...virgin-taker!''

Stunned, Paul watched as she stormed into the bedroom and viciously slammed the door. For a minute he did nothing but stand with a book and salt-shaker in his hand, too bemused to move. Beyond her explosive fury, what shocked Paul most was the incredible hurt he saw in her eyes.

"Virgin-taker?" he repeated in an astonished whisper.

Inside the bedroom, Caroline sat on the edge of the mattress. Stinging tears threatened to run down her face and she rubbed the heels of her hands against her eyes in a futile effort to restrain their salty release. Damn it all, she was falling in love with him—head over heels in love with a man without morals or conscience. If she didn't love him, then knowing what he'd done wouldn't hurt this much. Caroline cried harder. She didn't want to love him. In time, he'd realize their marriage was a terrible mistake and would send her back to Seattle. Caroline wanted to leave Paul and Alaska without regrets. A hiccupping sob ripped through her throat and she buried her face in her hands.

Her crying had an overwhelming effect on Paul. He'd thought to wait until her anger had fully dissipated before trying to reason with her, but he couldn't. Every sob felt like a vicious punch in his abdomen.

"Caroline," he called softly from the other side of the door. "Can we talk about this?"

Silence.

"Caroline, believe me, I haven't the foggiest idea what you're talking about."

"I'll just bet you don't!"

"I don't." He tried the knob, but she'd locked the door. "As your husband, I demand that you open this door immediately."

She snickered.

"Caroline, I mean it." When she didn't respond, he rammed his hands in his pants pockets, not knowing what else to do. "Are you angry about our wedding night? Is that it?" Standing directly in front of the door, he braced his hands on each side of the jamb. "I can see it isn't going to do the least bit of good to try to talk to you now. You're in no mood to be reasonable."

With that, the bedroom door opened so unexpectedly that he almost fell through the doorway.

Caroline glared at him with renewed animosity. "Do you mean to tell me that . . . that on the night we were married you . . . you took advantage of me?"

"Caroline, if you'd listen . . ."

"O-o-h." Her clenched fists pommeled his rock-hard chest until her fingers felt numb with pain.

"That's enough." Paul caught her wrists and quickly pinned her against the wall. Her shoulders heaved with exertion, and tears streaked her face and brimmed in her wide, blue eyes.

Trembling, she collected herself and drew in a ragged breath. Briefly, she struggled to be free, but Paul's hold tightened. His fierce look held her as effectively as his hands. Caroline met his glare with open defiance.

"Love." His voice was a hoarse whisper of bewilderment and confusion, his face mere inches from her own. "What is it?"

He spoke with such gentleness, such caring that it would be so easy to forget what he was and what he'd done. "Let me loose," she begged, her rage gone now, replaced by a far deeper, more crippling emotion—sorrow.

Paul saw the pain in her eyes and was filled with such perplexity that he reacted instinctively. In an effort to comfort, his mouth sought hers.

"No," Caroline cried, twisting her head from side to side, but her renewed struggles were a puny effort against his far superior strength. With his muscular torso, he anchored her body against the wall.

"Yes," he returned. His mouth was insistent, demanding, relentless, moving over hers with practiced ease. Caroline wanted to fight him, but the battle was one she couldn't hope to win and against her will she found her lips parting to meet his with an eagerness that rocked her soul. Their mouths twisted and turned almost cruelly against each other's in an urgent, fiery tempest of uncertainty and confusion. Gradually they relaxed, the crucial need abated. Paul loosened his grip, but continued to hold her wrists to the wall. His torso, warm from the struggle, secured her against him and Caroline became aware of the heavy thud of his heart while her own pulsed with a frantic rhythm.

They breathed in unison. Paul's gaze searched her face, looking for any clue that would help him understand her irrational behavior. Hot color stained her cheeks, but he didn't know if it was from her anger or her attempts to be free of him. Her lips were moist, dewy from his kisses, and he dipped his head to sample again their intoxicating sweetness. When he finally drew back, they were both trembling.

He released her hands and Caroline dropped them to her side. "I was with the women today," she began, in a voice so fraught with pain that Paul wrapped her securely in his arms. "And they told me..."

"Told you what, love?"

"That...you're a fantastic lover."

He frowned. "Ah," he whispered slowly, and cupped her face with his hands, kissing her briefly. "And you assumed they meant it literally?"

"How else was I supposed to take it?"

"Love, you must remember their culture is different from our own. I've been with them several years now. They know me well enough to favor me with certain attributes they *believe* I possess."

Caroline's gaze hungrily searched his, seeking the truth. "They sounded so...so knowledgeable."

He grinned widely. "Love, I'm only one man. I couldn't possibly have had that many lovers."

"Have you had...even one?" Her intense gaze locked with his.

"By everything I hold dear, I swear to you that I've never had a single lover from Atta." Paul had assumed that she would welcome his assurance, but his words produced the most uncanny response; tears flooded her eyes and streamed down her face. Caroline hugged him fiercely, burying her face in his sweater. Half laughing, half crying, she lifted her head then and spread eager kisses mingled with salty tears upon his face. Gently, Paul held her, wondering if he'd been so long outside civilization that he'd lost his ability to understand women. He sighed; perhaps he had.

Their relationship altered after that night. The changes were subtle ones and came about so naturally that Paul could only guess their meaning. The first thing he noticed was that Caroline had placed her suitcase under the bed as though she had finally accepted her position in his life and planned to remain. He yearned for her to do away with the idea that someday he would release her and she'd return to Seattle.

He knew she spent a lot of time with Tanana and apparently the two had worked out an agreement concerning dinner since Caroline started cooking all their meals. She'd once told him she was an excellent cook and he found that she hadn't exaggerated. She was clever, inventive and resourceful. It wasn't every woman who could make dried eggs edible.

Everyone was her friend; even Walter Thundercloud had become her ally. Paul had been in the village six months before the old man had fully accepted him. Walter's acceptance was typical of the love given Caroline by all the natives of Atta. The children adored her; Caroline couldn't walk out the door without two or three of them running to her side, their eyes wide and curious. More often than not, Caroline had something in her pocket just for them—a stick of gum, a marble or two or a whistle. One day Paul discovered Caroline in the meeting hall, skipping rope with the sixth-grade girls. Another day he found her involved in a heated soccer game with the junior-high boys.

When an old woman had a toothache, she came to Caroline. A feverish baby was brought to her as well. A little boy with a side ache showed up unexpectedly one afternoon. The medical clinic was open once a week when a team from the Public Health Department flew in for appointments, but it was Caroline whom the villagers came to.

She was gentle and kind and Paul was so much in love he thought he'd die from wanting her. To rush her into lovemaking now would be foolish. She was so close to recognizing she loved him, and when that day came it would be right and beautiful, although he often wondered how much longer he could hold out. He endured the sweetest torture each morning when he woke up to find her in his arms. At night, the agony was far greater; he dreaded her touch and at the same time craved it.

That evening after dinner, Caroline brought out a large box and placed it on the ottoman in front of him.

Paul lowered the two-day-old newspaper and raised questioning eyes to his wife. "What's this?"

"Open it and see." Her face revealed her anxiety. She'd worked so hard and so long on this sweater that if it didn't fit, she'd burst into tears. "I probably should have saved it for Christmas, but..." It was silly to be this nervous, but she so wanted to please him and the holidays were a full six weeks away. Besides, she didn't know what else she could do to tell Paul she loved him.

"But what, love?"

"But I thought you deserved it now." For calming her angry tirades, for being so patient with her, for his gentleness and a hundred other admirable qualities. And because she longed to be his wife in the truest sense of the word.

Carefully, Paul removed the top from the oblong box and lifted out the Irish cable-knit sweater. "Caroline, I'm . . . stunned; it's a fine piece of work."

"If it doesn't fit, I can redo it." She couldn't believe she'd made that offer; the pattern was both difficult and complicated. If it hadn't been for Tanana's and the other women's help, she would have given up and thrown the sweater away weeks before.

"I'm sure it will fit perfectly." To prove his point, he stood and placed it over his head, slipping his arms into the long sleeves. "Where did you get the yarn?" he asked, running his hand over the finely crafted garment. It was a lovely shade of winter wheat and far lighter than the material the village women used.

"I mailed away for it. Mary Finefeather had a catalog."

"How did you pay for it?" She'd never come to him for money, although he would have been more than pleased to give it to her. They had little need for cash in Atta. The supply store and grocery mailed him monthly accounts and his paychecks were automatically deposited in the Fairbanks Savings and Loan.

"I used my traveler's checks."

He nodded and kissed her lightly. "Thank you, love. I'll always treasure it."

Caroline's returning smile was weak, as though she was greatly disappointed by his response. Paul watched her leave and wondered if he'd said something to offend her. He began to doubt that he'd ever understand her.

Hours later, Paul lay at her side. His even breathing convinced Caroline he was sound asleep as she lay on her back wide-eyed, staring at the ceiling. She was now convinced that she was a terrible failure. For two weeks, she'd been trying to tell Paul that she was ready to be his wife in *every* way. How one man could be so completely blind was beyond her. If it hadn't been for a few occasional looks of longing he'd secretly given her, she would have abandoned her cause. She made excuses to be close to him, touch him. The signals she'd been sending him would have stopped a freight train! The sweater had been her ace in the hole and even that had failed. In return, he'd kissed her like an affectionate older brother.

Ah well, there was always another day. Maybe if she wore the fur-trimmed nightgown her aunts had given her... She smiled and her eyes drifted closed. She couldn't get any more obvious than that.

The next day was a busy one. The small town was holding an early Thanksgiving feast, and it seemed half of Alaska had been invited. People had been arriving from the outlying areas all morning. Caroline and Tanana were responsible for decorating the meeting hall and the two of them made a comical sight. Caroline wouldn't allow Tanana, who was in the advanced stages of pregnancy, to climb the ladder to hang the crepe paper streamers, so Caroline wrapped them around her neck and hauled them up herself.

"This isn't fair," Tanana complained. "All I'm doing is holding the ladder for you."

"I'm not going to let you stand on this rickety old thing," Caroline muttered, stretching as far as her limbs would allow to stick the thumbtack into the beam.

"If Mr. Trevor ever saw this, he'd be plumb mad."

"He isn't going to know, and you're not going to tell him—right?"

"What will you bribe me with?"

Caroline laughed. Her young friend was quickly learning the ways of the world. "Hush, now, and hand me another streamer." She climbed down a couple of steps and Tanana gave her the next set of bright red crepe paper strips.

When they had finished, the two women looked about them, proud of their accomplishment. It was amazing what a little bit of color did to add to the festive spirit.

Mary Finefeather, a foster grandmother to many of the village youth, delivered sandwiches to Caroline and Tanana. Typical of the older woman's personality, Mary spoke in choppy one-word sentences.

"Eat," she said with a toothy grin.

"I think that's an order," Caroline commented, and looked to Tanana, who smiled in reply. The younger girl had lost much of her shyness now and Caroline considered her a valued friend.

"What you getting Mr. Trevor for Christmas?" Tanana questioned, studying Caroline with dark, soulful eyes.

"I...don't know. I gave him the sweater last night."
She wished she hadn't; with the holidays fast approaching, she had wasted her best gift—seemingly for naught.

"I know what Mr. Trevor wants."

"You do?"

Tanana placed her hand on her swollen abdomen and stared at her stomach. "Mr. Trevor wants son."

Caroline nearly swallowed her sandwich whole. "Oh?"

"You'll give him many fine sons?"

Embarrassed, Caroline looked away. "Someday."

"Soon?" the girl pressed.

"I...I don't know." Caroline couldn't very well announce that she and Paul had never made love, at least not so as she could remember.

Caroline worked for part of the afternoon, then returned to the cabin, frustrated and tired. She'd slept poorly the night before and tonight would be another late one as well. Before she could talk herself out of the idea, she climbed on top of the bed and closed her eyes, intending to rest for only a few minutes.

Paul found her there an hour later, barely visible in the soft light of dusk. He paused in the doorway of their bedroom and experienced such a wave of desire that he sucked in a tight breath. Her blouse had ridden up to expose the creamy smooth skin of her midriff. Her ripe breasts were cupped in a mere piece of white lace. Paul's hands clenched at his sides with the intense yearning to weigh her breasts in his hands and know for himself the taste of their delicate pink crests. He'd been patient, more than patient. Blood pounded in his head and his feet seemed to move of their own accord, taking him to her side. Just to see her like this was enough to make him tipsy with desire.

His gaze lingered on the smooth slant of her brow and a smile briefly touched his intense features. She could make a clearer statement with an arch of her eyebrow than some women said in twenty years. Her nose was perfect and her sweet, firm lips were enough to drive a man insane. She tasted of honey and wine and one sampling was never enough. He thought about the last time they'd kissed and how, for hours afterward, he'd been in a foul mood, barking at Walter Thundercloud and the others until Walter had suggested that Paul do something to cure whatever was ailing him.

Caroline was ailing him. She was in his blood, a cancer that was eating away at him inch by inch. She was his wife, and by God, he'd . . .

Caroline yawned and rolled over.

Paul jumped away from her as though he'd been burned. His knees felt like pudding, his heart like slush in a spring thaw. On unsteady feet, he walked over to the dresser.

"Caroline, it's time to get up." He hardly recognized the strained, harsh voice as his own.

Slowly, she opened her eyes. She'd been having the most incredibly wonderful dream about giving Paul the son Tanana claimed he wanted so badly. One look at her husband, who stood stiffly on the other side of the room, was enough to return her into the cold world of reality. His back was to her.

"Hi," she said, stretching her hands high above her head and yawning loudly.

"Hi," he returned gruffly. He didn't dare turn around. If her midriff had been showing before, God only knew what he'd glimpse now. He felt himself go weak all over again.

Caroline frowned at his abruptness. "Did you have a good day?"

"Sure." He pulled open the top drawer and took out a clean T-shirt. "You'd better get dressed or we'll be late for the party."

"What time is it?"

"Five."

Caroline's frown deepened. No one was expected before seven. "We've got plenty of time."

No, we don't, Paul wanted to shout. He, for one, was at the end of his rope.

"Paul, what's wrong?"

"Nothing." He slammed the drawer shut with unnecessary force. "I just happen to think it was time you got out of bed."

"Are you angry because I took a nap?"

"No," he barked.

She rose to a sitting position and released a long sigh. "Sometimes I don't understand you."

"That makes two of us."

"Will you please turn around? I don't like talking to your back." She made the request softly, confused by his harsh mood. She'd never known Paul to be so short-tempered and illogical.

"If you don't mind, I'm busy."

Caroline blinked, stunned. The conversation with Tanana played back in her mind and a heaviness settled on her shoulders. She loved Paul and yearned to give him a child, but instead of growing together they seemed to be drifting apart. Sudden tears misted her eyes. She'd thought that once she acknowledged that she was in love with him everything would be perfect. Instead, it had gotten worse—much worse.

Paul tossed his sweater on the bed. "Good grief, don't tell me you're crying! One day you're hurling saltshakers at me and the next you're weeping because I tell you to hurry and get ready for a party you've been working on all day."

Her eyes rounded with determination to hold back the tears. "I'm not crying. That's ridiculous. Why should I be crying?"

He threw up his hands. "God only knows. I've given up trying to understand you."

The party was a grand success; the meeting hall burst to the rafters with friends and loved ones from nearby communities. The dinner proved to be scrumptious and Caroline received rave reviews for her apple pies and decorating efforts. Although she smiled and made all the appropriate responses, she couldn't seem to get into the party mood.

When the tables were cleared and the dancing began, Caroline noted how Paul seemed to dance with every woman in the room but her. Not that Caroline was given much time to notice. One partner after another claimed her hand for a turn around the floor.

After an hour, she pleaded exhaustion and sat down, fanning her flushed face with one hand.

To her surprise, Paul joined her, sitting in the chair beside her own. His mouth was pinched, his face grim. "I imagine you're pleased to have every man for a hundred miles panting after you."

Caroline's mouth fell open at the unjust accusation. Quickly, she composed herself, stiffening her back. "I'm going to forgive you for that remark, Paul Trevor, because I owe you one. But from here on we're even." She stood and purposely walked away from him. Blinded by confusion, she nearly stumbled into Walter Thundercloud, and glancing up at him, hurriedly stammered an apology.

"Didn't you promise me this dance?" Walter said.

Still unable to find her tongue, Caroline nodded.

Studying her, the Athabascan guided her onto the dance floor. A waltz was playing and Caroline lightly slipped one arm around the older man's neck and placed her hand in his.

"All right, girl, tell me—what's made you so unhappy?"

Caroline's mouth formed a poor excuse for a smile. "Paul. I don't know how any one man can be so stupid."

"He's blinded with his love for you."

"I sincerely doubt that's it." Caroline gazed directly into the blunt Indian features. "I have the feeling he's ready to ship me back to Seattle." There had been a time when she'd prayed for exactly that, but now her heart ached at the mere thought of leaving him.

Standing by the punch bowl, Paul watched her. Caroline could feel his dark gaze on her back. With every passing minute, his eyes grew darker and more angry.

Walter chuckled, the sound coming deep from within his throat. "Paul would rather cut off his arm than send you away. Have you told him you love him?"

Caroline's shocked gaze clashed with the man's wise old eyes. "No."

"Then do it, and soon, before he makes an even bigger fool of himself."

When the dance ended, Walter delivered her to Paul's side and quietly left them. Caroline and Paul stood glaring at each other until the music started.

"Shall we?" Caroline asked, glancing toward the crowded floor.

"Why not? You've seen fit to dance with every other male here tonight."

"Paul," she whispered. "Are you jealous?"

He didn't answer her, but she noted that his features were as grim and tight as she'd ever seen them. His hold on her was loose, as though he couldn't bear to touch her.

Caroline swallowed her pride. "There isn't anyone here that I'd rather dance with more than you."

Still, he said nothing. His eyes were focused straight ahead and there wasn't so much as a flicker in his rock-hard features to indicate that he'd heard her, or if he had that her words had had any effect on him.

"When I first came to Atta, I hated it."

If possible, his mouth grew harder, more inflexible.

"But . . . things changed and I realized I was happy here. There's a wildness to this land. A challenge that makes people strong and wise. I've seen that in you and admired your patience and gentleness."

Momentarily, Paul dropped his gaze and studied her as though he didn't quite trust what she was saying.

Caroline thought her heart would burst with pain when he quickly glanced away, dismissing her claim.

"You idiot," she hissed and brought her shoe down hard on the top of his foot.

Paul let out a small yelp of pain.

"I'm trying to tell you I love you, but you can forget it. And while you're at it, you can forget about our son, too!" Forcefully, she broke away and left him holding up one leg like a flamingo while he nursed his injured foot.

At the door, Caroline grabbed her boots and parka and stormed out of the meeting hall, too angry for tears, too frustrated to think what she was doing. She knew only that she had to escape.

"Caroline!"

His frantic call came to her before she reached the cabin door. With stiff resolve, she chose to pretend she hadn't heard him.

"Damn it, Caroline, would you wait?"

She ignored his pleading as well. By the time he arrived home, she was sitting in front of the fireplace with a book in front of her face, studiously focusing her attention on the fine print.

"Caroline...what did you just say?" He was breathless, his voice rushed and uneven.

"It was nothing."

"It was everything," he whispered in awe. "Do you love me? Caroline, for God's sake would you kindly look at me?"

"No."

Paul felt like he was going to explode with happiness. "And what was that crazy remark about a son?"

She turned the page of the novel and glanced with keen interest at the beginning of the next chapter, although she hadn't a clue as to the story line.

Paul fell to his knees at her side and removed the book from her stiff fingers. Her eyes refused to meet his, although his looked demanded it of her. "Caroline..." He breathed her name with a heart overflowing with expectancy and hope. "Oh God, are you telling me you're ready to be my wife?"

"I couldn't have made it any plainer. I've flaunted myself like a hussy in front of you all week. I gave you the sweater...hoping... Paul Trevor, you're an idiot! For days, I've been throwing myself at you and you...you've been so blind and so stupid."

"You have?" Paul was flabbergasted. "When? Days?"

"Weeks!"

"Weeks?" Dear God, he had been blind, but no longer.

His hands framed her face as he guided her lips to his, kissing her with such hungry intensity it robbed her breath. Without her being aware of how he managed it, he lifted her from the chair, cradled her in his arms and carried her into their bedroom. He laid her upon the mattress and knelt over her, studying her once more to be sure this wasn't some dream.

Caroline stared into his hungry eyes and twined her arms around his neck, bringing his mouth back to her own to kiss him long and ardently. "You idiot," she whispered.

"No more, love."

Their lips met again and again as though each kiss was sweeter and more potent than the one before. Holding back nothing, Caroline surrendered to him with joyful abandon. He explored her face and her neck, charting undiscovered territory with his lips as he helped her undress. Finally they were both free of restricting clothes and Paul kissed her until she responded with a wantonness she didn't know she possessed. They broke apart, winded and panting.

"Caroline," he murmured, his features keen and ardent in the moonlight. "Are you sure?"

"I've never been more sure of anything in my life."

Utterly content, Caroline lay with her cheek pressed against her husband's chest. Her silken leg stroked his and she sighed her happiness. There was no turning back for them now; they were truly husband and wife, their commitment to each other complete.

Paul's hand smoothed the tumbled hair from her face. "Are you happy, love?"

"Very." Her nails playfully scraped at his curling chest hairs. "Why didn't you tell me it was this good? If I'd known, I would have demanded my wifely rights." She lifted her head to kiss the strong, proud line of his chin. "The Athabascan women were right; you are a fantastic lover."

Paul opened his mouth to answer her when there was a loud knock on the front door. Caroline gave him a look of dismay; no one would come unless there was trouble.

Paul rolled to his feet, his body tense and alert. "I'll be right back." He reached for his clothes and was gone before she could protest.

Caroline dressed in a rush, anxious now. When she joined Paul in the living room, she found him speaking hurriedly to Thomas Eagleclaw, Tanana's young husband.

"Tanana's gone into labor," Paul explained. "Her mother is with her, but she wants you."

Caroline nodded. "I won't be a minute."

Chapter Seven

By the time Caroline arrived at Tanana's cabin, her heart was pounding, not with exertion from the long walk, but with excitement and, she admitted, anxiety. Her experience had been limited to a sterile hospital delivery room with a doctor, other nurses and all the necessary emergency equipment. None of that existed in Atta, and Caroline had never felt more inadequate.

Thomas, Tanana's husband, led the way into their cabin, which was even smaller than Paul's. Tanana lay in the center of the double bed, her face glistening with perspiration, her eyes wide with pain. The Indian girl held her hand out to Caroline. "Thank you for coming."

"When did the pains start?" Caroline asked, sitting on the edge of the mattress.

Tanana lowered her gaze. "This afternoon."

"Why didn't you tell me?"

"I wasn't sure they were true."

Caroline understood. Tanana had mentioned twice that week that she'd been experiencing "twinges" in her abdomen. Caroline had explained that those were normal and the girl needn't worry.

The older Indian in the bedroom rose to greet the latest arrival. Caroline had met Tanana's mother previously and the older woman smiled her welcome and returned to her rocking chair, content to let Caroline assume the role of midwife. Wonderful, Caroline mused dryly, returning to the kitchen to wash her hands. Silently, she prayed this would be an easy birth, routine in every way.

It wasn't. Hours later, both Caroline and Tanana were drenched with sweat. The girl was terrified. Caroline, although outwardly calm, was equally frightened. Tanana's mother continued to rock, offering an encouraging smile now and again. Certainly the old Indian had delivered countless babies, Caroline thought.

"It shouldn't be long now," Caroline said, smoothing the hair from Tanana's brow and wiping her face with a cool washcloth.

The Indian girl tried to smile, but the effort was too great. "Rest as much as you can between pains," Caroline instructed.

Tanana nodded. She closed her eyes and rolled her head to the side, ruthlessly biting into the corner of her lip as another contraction took hold of her young body.

"Don't fight it," Caroline said softly. "Try to deal with the pain."

Tanana's death grip on Caroline's fingers slacked and Caroline relaxed as well. "You're doing great, Tanana. I'll check you with the next contraction and we'll see how far things have progressed."

Caroline's worst fears were confirmed; the baby was breech. The knot of fear that clogged her throat was palpable. Didn't this baby realize she had only limited experience in this area? The least it could do was cooperate! "I'm going to get some fresh water," she told Tanana, and stood to leave the bedside. Tanana's eyes revealed her fear. "Don't worry," Caroline said with a reassuring smile, "I'll be right back."

In the next room, Paul was playing cards with Thomas, although it was easy to see that neither man's attention was on the game. One look at Caroline's distraught eyes and Paul stood and moved to her side at the kitchen sink. "What's wrong?"

"The baby is breech. Paul, I'm frightened. This is far more complicated than anything I've ever handled. Good Lord, I've worked in a doctor's office for two years; you don't get much experience in delivering breech babies in an office building."

"Tanana needs you."

"I know." Paul was referring to strength and confidence, but she couldn't offer the poor girl something she didn't have herself.

"If it becomes more than you can cope with, we'll call in a plane and fly her to Fairbanks."

That would take hours and they both knew it. "I'll...do my best."

"I know you will, love." Gently, his hands cupped her face and he kissed her, his lips fitting tenderly over hers, lending her his own strength. A whimper from Tanana broke them apart and Caroline hurried back to her friend's side.

The hours sped by, but Caroline was barely aware of their passing. She was busy every minute, talking softly, encouraging Tanana. Her friend's fortitude and inner strength amazed her. Several times, Caroline thought Tanana would succumb to the pain and fear. When the squalling infant was released from the young girl's body, unrestrained tears of happiness filled Caroline's eyes.

"You have a son," she said, gently placing the baby atop his mother's stomach.

"A son." Tanana's wide smile revealed her overwhelming delight and with a cry of joy, she fell back against the pillow, content for the moment.

A few minutes later, Caroline entered the kitchen, carrying the crying infant in her arms. Her eyes met Paul's as the two men slowly rose to their feet.

"A boy," she said softly.

Thomas let out a hoot of exhilarated happiness and paused to briefly inspect his son before he rushed past Caroline to join his wife.

Paul looked down at the small bundle in her arms. His eyes softened at the wrinkled face and tiny fingers protruding from the soft blanket. "You must be exhausted," he said, studying Caroline.

Lightly, she shook her head. She'd never experienced such a wondrous feeling of excited bliss in her life. It was as though she'd labored for this child herself and he had been born of her own body. "He's so beautiful." Unabashed tears filled her eyes and she kissed the baby's sweet brow.

"Not half as beautiful as you, love," Paul said tenderly, his heart constricting at the sight of a babe in his wife's arms. The day would come when they would bear a child of their own and the thought filled him with happy anticipation.

An hour later, when both mother and baby were resting comfortably, Paul took Caroline back to their cabin. Now that the first surge of high spirits had faded, Caroline realized how weary she was. "What time is it?"

"Noon."

"Noon? Really?"

Paul led her directly into their bedroom and sat her down on the bed where she fell back upon the rumpled sheets and heaved a sigh, closing her eyes. Smiling down on her, Paul removed her shoes.

"Paul?"

"Hmm?" He unzipped her jeans next and slid them from her long legs. A surge of desire shot through him and he forced himself to look at her face and remember how exhausted she was. Given the least amount of encouragement, he would have fallen into bed beside her.

"Tanana told me you wanted a son." Her eyes were closed and she felt weary and lethargic, as though someone had drugged her.

"A daughter would do as well."

"Soon?"

"Sooner than you think if you don't get under those covers," he grumbled, lifting the thick quilts over his wife's inviting body.

Caroline smiled, feeling warm and unbelievably secure. "I love you," she murmured dreamily.

The words rocked Paul. He stood at the edge of the bed, unsteady. "You love me?" He'd only dared to dream her love would come this soon. She didn't answer him and he knew that she was already asleep. His heart swelled with such joy that he felt like shouting and dancing around the small room. Instead, he bent down and gently kissed her temple. To remain with her now would be torture and although it was a different kind of agony, Paul left the room and curled up on the recliner, meaning only to rest his eyes.

Caroline found him there several hours later. "Paul," she whispered, lightly shaking his shoulder.

With much reluctance, he opened his eyes. When he saw it was Caroline, he grinned sleepily. "Did you rest?"

"Like a baby. Why are you curled up out here?"

"Because you needed your rest, love." His arm circled her waist and brought her into his lap where he nuzzled her neck. She felt incredibly good in his arms, soft, feminine, his—all his. He owned her heart now. Larry was in the past and gone forever.

Paul thought of his life before she'd come to him and wondered how he'd managed all those years without her. She was as much a part of him now as his own heart. She was his world, his sun, his pride all in one. All these weeks she'd led him down a rock-strewn trail, but every minute had been worth the wait. She was more than he'd ever dreamed.

Her hands directed his mouth to hers and she kissed him hungrily. He didn't need to tell her why he'd slept on the recliner; Caroline knew and loved him all the more for his thoughtfulness.

"Oh Lord, Caroline," he groaned, his mouth repeatedly rubbing over hers. "Do you know what you're doing?"

She answered him by unfastening the buttons of his shirt and slipping her fingers inside to stroke his chest. The wild sensations he aroused in her were so exquisite, she wanted to weep.

The soft gentle sounds of their lovemaking filled the cabin. Whispered phrases of awe followed as Paul removed her blouse and freed her breasts.

"Caroline," he moaned, his voice low and husky. "If we don't stop right now, we're going to end up making love in this recliner."

"I'm not willing to stop...."

In the days that followed, Caroline was astonished that they'd waited so long to become lovers when everything was so extraordinarily right between them. Now they seemed to be making up for lost time. His desire for her both delighted and astonished Caroline. They made love every night and often Paul couldn't seem to wait until their usual bedtime. In the middle of a Scrabble game, she found him looking at her with a fierce gleam in his eye.

"Paul?"

He glanced toward the bedroom and arched his brows in question.

"It's only seven o'clock," she said, laughing with a hint of disbelief.

His look was almost boyish as he dropped his gaze. "I can wait."

Caroline smiled, stood and walked around the table to take him by the hand. "Well, I can't."

They never finished playing Scrabble. Instead they invented new games.

Some nights, Paul was barely in the door when he wanted her.

"What's for dinner?" he would ask.

She'd tell him and catch that look in his eye and automatically turn down the stove. "Don't worry, it can simmer for an hour."

Their dinner simmered and they sizzled. This was the honeymoon they never had and Caroline prayed it would last a lifetime.

She yearned to get pregnant, but the first week of December, she discovered sadly that she wasn't.

"If the truth be known," Paul said comfortingly, "I'd rather have you to myself for a little while."

Caroline nestled close to his side, her head in the crook of his arm. "It may not be so easy for me. My mother had a difficult time getting pregnant."

"Then we'll just have to work at it, love."

Caroline laughed; if they worked any harder, they would drop from sheer exhaustion. Paul kissed her and held her close. "I never thought I'd find such happiness," he told her.

"Me either." He wasn't a man of many words, not one for flowery speeches. Nor did he shower her with expensive gifts. But his actions were far more effective than mere words. He loved her, and every day he did something to let her know how much he cared.

One morning after Paul had left for work, Caroline realized that she'd nearly let all this happiness slip through her fingers. The pain of Larry's rejection had nearly blinded her to Paul's love. When Larry had left, Caroline had almost died inside. Now she realized how mismatched they had been. They'd been friends, good friends, and erroneously had assumed a friendship as strong as theirs meant they would automatically be good lovers. It wasn't until she and Paul became lovers that Caroline could acknowledge that a marriage to Larry would have been a terrible mistake. Only Larry had recognized the cold hard facts.

Undoubtedly, Larry was torturing himself with guilt. Her aunts had mentioned his visit in a letter and although his name was only brought up briefly again, Caroline knew that he'd been back to visit her aunts, hungry for word of her.

In an effort to ease her friend's mind, Caroline decided to write Larry a letter. It was the least she could do. He'd feel better and she could tell him herself how happy she was. She wished him the best and was eternally grateful that he'd had the wisdom and the courage to keep them both from making a colossal mistake.

Caroline had originally intended her letter to be brief, but by the time she'd finished, she'd written five notebook pages. She told him about Paul and how much she loved her husband and thanked Larry for being her friend. She added bits and pieces about her life in Alaska and how marvelous the land was. Come summer, Paul had promised to take her hiking and fishing and she joked with Larry because he got queasy at the sight of a worm. When she'd finished, Caroline read the letter and realized that her happiness shone through like a beacon. Larry would have no more doubts.

After stuffing the five pages into an envelope, Caroline carried the letter over to the supply store that also served as the local post office.

"Good afternoon, Harry," she greeted the proprietor with a ready smile.

"Mrs. Trevor," he returned formally. "Nice day, isn't it?"

"It's a beautiful day." She handed him the letter.

"This all I can do for you?"

Caroline hedged. "It is unless you can sell me a pizza. I've had the craving for a thick, cheesy pizza all week."

He chuckled and rubbed the side of his jaw. "Unless there's a frozen one at the grocery, I'd say you're out of luck."

"I had that feeling," she grumbled, and with a cheery wave, was gone.

Paul rounded the corner of the supply store just as Caroline disappeared. "Afternoon, Harry. Was that my wife?"

"Yup, you just missed her. She came to mail a letter."

Paul's gaze sought Caroline out, but she was too far away from him to shout.

"Thick letter too, now that I look at it. She might be needing an extra stamp. I best weigh it."

Paul nodded, hardly hearing the man. "She's fond of those aunts of hers."

"Her aunt has a funny name then: Larry Atkins."

The name sliced through Paul as effectively as the serrated edge of a knife. He attempted to hide his shock and anger from Harry, but doubted that he had. Without bothering to buy what he'd needed, Paul left soon afterward and returned to the pumping station. He tried reasoning with himself that it was only a letter, then he recalled all the times Caroline had walked letters over to Harry, preferring to deliver them herself, claiming she needed the exercise.

His anger only increased when he remembered how she'd sat at the desk across from his own and vowed to find a means of escaping him. Her voice had been filled with conviction and vengeance. In his callowness, Paul hadn't expected her to be so deceitful. Once he was putty in her hands, she'd silently slip away.

"That's ridiculous," Paul said aloud. "No woman is that good an actress."

All the talk of a child. Dear Lord, she knew his Achilles' heel. He sat at his desk and slumped forward, burying his face in his hands. He couldn't condemn her on such flimsy evidence, but he couldn't trust her either. She'd taught him that once when she'd walked out on him with Burt Manners, but it seemed he was a slow learner.

By the time Paul arrived home that evening, he was, to all appearances, outwardly calm.

Caroline whirled around when he entered the cabin. "Guess what I'm making for dinner." Her smile was brighter than the sun had been all day.

"What's that, love?"

"Pizza."

"Pizza?"

"Well, a close facsimile. I didn't have a round pan so I'm using a square one. And I didn't want to make bread dough, so I'm making do with biscuit batter. And last but not least, we didn't have any sausage so I'm using ground caribou."

"A caribou pizza?"

"How does it sound?"

"Like we'll be eating scrambled eggs later."

"Oh, ye of little faith."

Paul laughed shortly; she didn't know the half of it.

Dinner was only partially successful. To her credit, the caribou pizza wasn't half bad. He managed to eat a piece and praised her ingenuity.

"What's for dinner tomorrow night? Moose Tacos?"

She laughed and promised him fried chicken.

While Caroline did the dishes, she watched Paul. He sat in the recliner with the paper resting in his lap as he stared into space. His face was so intent that she wondered what could be troubling him.

"Paul."

He shook himself from his reprieve.

"Is something wrong?"

"Nothing, love. I was just thinking."

"About what? You looked so pensive."

"Life." His grin was wry.

"Life?"

"It's taken an unexpected turn for us, hasn't it?" He eyed her carefully, hoping to read her heart and know for himself the truth. He saw the love and devotion shining from her eyes and called himself every kind of fool.

"Tanana let me watch Carl for her this afternoon," she announced, smiling. "He's growing so fast."

"You love that baby, don't you?"

"As much as if he were our own."

Tenderness wrapped its way around his heart, suffocating his doubts. He had Caroline as his own, loved her more than life itself. If she were playing him for a fool, then he was the happiest idiot alive. He planned to hold on to that contentment, hug it against his breast and treasure every minute she was with him for as long as it lasted. She might dream of her precious Larry, she might even write the bastard, but it was in the curve of his arm where she slept. It was his body that filled hers and gave her such pleasure that she wept with joy. It was his name she bore and later, God willing, it would be his children her slim body gave life to.

When they made love that night, it was like a storm of passion that had overtaken them. Electricity arced between them, the current more powerful than lightning. Each caress became a fire only their love could extinguish. Gradually their love play crescendoed into a rhapsody that rose ever upward, building, mount-

ing until it seemed that all the instruments in the world
had joined together for one joyous song. Afterward,
Caroline lay limp and drowsy in her husband's arms.
Her cheeks were flushed with the gentle blush of pleasure, her breath uneven. Paul closed his eyes, wondering how he could have ever doubted her. He buried
his face in her hair, savoring the fragrance, and held
her close until he recognized the even meter of her
breathing and knew she was dreaming.

Caroline wasn't sure what woke her. One minute she
was asleep and the next awake. It took her a moment
to realize Paul wasn't asleep.

"Paul, what's wrong?"

"Not a thing, love."

She slipped her hand over his ribs and buried her
face in his throat. He'd been so quiet this evening and
their lovemaking had been a desperate act of passion.
Paul wasn't himself and Caroline wondered what had
happened to bring this about. "I've failed you in some
way, haven't I?"

He hesitated. "No, love, I fear I may have failed
you."

"Paul, no. I'm happy, truly happy."

"Do you miss Seattle?"

"I miss my aunts," she admitted. "I wish you could
meet them; they're a delight. And now and then I
think about my friends, but there's nothing for me in
Seattle now that I'm with you."

"I love you, Caroline."

She smiled and kissed the side of his mouth. He'd
shown her his love in a hundred ways, but he'd never
said the words. "I know."

"You're laughing at me, aren't you?" His grip on her tightened as though he wished to punish her.

Caroline jerked away from him with a gasp. "Paul, what's gotten into you?"

He held himself rigid and didn't speak for an interminable moment. "I told you I loved you and I know you were smiling."

"I...was happy." She lay on her stomach, her hands buried under her.

Another long minute passed. "I'm sorry, love. I didn't mean to frighten you."

She nodded and rolled away from him. Their happiness was shattering right in front of her eyes and she was powerless to change it.

"Caroline," he said at last, reaching for her. "I talked to Harry after you were in the store today. I saw the letter you'd written to Larry Atkins."

Her brows arched. "It's obvious you didn't read it."

"Why?"

"If you had, your reaction would be altogether different."

"Have you written him in the past?" Paul hated his jealousy. All day he'd been brooding; furious with himself and unreasonable with Caroline. If love did this to a man, he wanted no part of it, and yet he wouldn't, couldn't give her up.

"This is my first letter to him."

"Why did you feel it was necessary to contact him now?"

"To thank him."

"What?"

"It's true. You mean this is what's been troubling you all day?"

He didn't answer, ashamed of his behavior.

"Why didn't you ask me earlier? I would have told you all about it. I wrote Larry to let him know he'd done me a gigantic favor by standing me up at the altar."

"You told him that?"

"Not exactly in those words, but basically that was what I said."

"Why didn't you tell me about writing him?"

Caroline expelled her breath on a nervous sigh. "To be truthful, I didn't think about it. My mistake. Are you always going to be this irrational?"

"When it comes to my wife contacting another man, you're damn right I am."

"It isn't like you're making it sound."

"I have only your word for that."

Caroline fumed, and rather than argue, she turned her back on him. "Good night, Paul," she grumbled. It wouldn't do any good to talk to him now. In the morning things would be better.

For two days they put the incident behind them. Their happiness was too complete to be destroyed over a silly letter and they each, independently, seemed to realize it. On the third day, Paul arrived home two hours before his usual time.

"You're home early." In the midst of writing out Christmas cards, she was delighted to see her husband.

He sat at the table across from her. "I've got to fly into Fairbanks for a few days."

"Oh, Paul, Fairbanks? Oh, heavens, I can hardly wait! The first thing I'm going to do is order a real sausage pizza with extra cheese and then I'm going to shop for twelve hours nonstop. You have no idea how much I wanted to buy Tanana and the baby something special for Christmas and there just doesn't seem to be anything in the catalogs. Why didn't you say something earlier?"

"Because..."

"And you know what else I'm going to do?" She answered her own question before he had the chance, her voice animated and high-pitched. "I'm going to soak in a hot bubble bath until my skin wilts, and watch television. Doesn't that sound silly?"

"Caroline," he said gruffly, his gaze just avoiding hers. "This is a business trip; I hadn't planned to bring you along."

Chapter Eight

It took a full minute for the words to sink into Caroline's baffled mind. "You're not taking me with you?" With deliberate patience, she set the pen down and pushed the Christmas cards aside. "Why?"

Paul refused to meet her probing gaze. "I've already explained that it was a business trip."

"That's not the reason and you know it, Paul Trevor." She'd thought they'd come so far, but the only one who had moved had been her. She'd walked into his arms and been so blinded by her love she hadn't recognized the chains that bound her.

"I don't know what you're talking about."

"Like hell!"

"I go to Fairbanks every other month or so...."

"Every other month?"

"You can go another time."

"I want to go now."

"No!"

"Why not?" She grew more furious by the moment.

"Because—"

"Because you saw that stupid letter to Larry and are absolutely convinced I've made arrangements to escape."

"Don't be ridiculous." But her accusation was so close to the truth that Paul's heart pounded hard against his ribs in silent objection.

Caroline's smile was sad. "Since I'm your prisoner, you might as well lock me in a cell."

"You're my wife!"

"I'm the woman who was forced into staying married to you. What we have isn't a marriage!" She saw him open his mouth to contradict her, then close it again. "It takes more than a piece of paper signed by the proper authorities to constitute a marriage."

"Caroline, you're making too much of this."

"Yes, master," she said, staring straight ahead, refusing to look at him. "Whatever you say, master." She gave him a mocking bow, folding her hands in front of her and bending low.

"Caroline, stop that."

"Anything you ask, master." He wanted a slave. Fine! She would give him one. She'd speak only when spoken to, bow to his every wish, smother him with her servitude.

Her unflagging calmness shocked her. It was as though the sun had come out in full force, revealing all the glaring imperfections of their relationship. She stared at the flaws, appalled and saddened. She'd come to love Paul and Alaska. She'd found happiness with him only to discover it was marred with imperfections. She was no better off now than she had been that first week when he'd forced her into becoming his shadow. The only difference was that she'd grown more comfortable in her cell.

Another thought came to her and she forgot her resolve not to speak. "How...how do I know you don't have a lover in Fairbanks?"

Paul stood, pushing back the kitchen chair with such force that it threatened to topple. "That's ridiculous. I can't believe you'd even think such a thing!"

"Why? I've lived with you these last two months, I'm well aware of your appetite for..."

"The only lover I have is you!" He shouted the words and stuffed his hands inside his pants pockets.

"If you can't trust me, there's nothing that says I have to trust you." She didn't think for a minute that Paul did have another woman, but she wanted him to sample a taste of her own frustration. "The fact you don't want me along speaks for itself. It's obvious you're hiding something from me." She arched her brows speculatively. "Another woman, no doubt."

Paul's mouth was tight. "That thought is unworthy of you."

"It's only tit for tat."

His expression darkened. "I'm leaving for Fairbanks and you're staying here and that's the way it's going to be."

Caroline fumed. "Yes, master."

"Oh, Lord, are we back to that?"

She didn't answer. Instead she walked across the cabin and reached for her parka and boots. "I'm going to see Tanana unless my master demands that I remain here."

"Caroline." He stopped her just before she opened the door, but she didn't turn around and Paul knew that she was fighting back tears. He felt himself go weak; he loved her and yearned to take away the pain, but it was too late to change his plans now. "Never mind," he said gruffly, and turned his back to her.

Caroline nodded and left him, gently closing the door behind her.

Paul paced the room, his thoughts in conflict. Caroline was right; she'd given him everything—her love, her heart, her trust... And yet, he wasn't satisfied; he wanted more.

The cold wind cut through Caroline as she traipsed the frozen pathway that led to the Eagleclaws' cabin. She needed to get away and think. Paul had hurt her; he'd never guess to what extent his doubts pained her sensitive heart. No matter how strenuously he argued otherwise, she was his prisoner in fact and in deed.

Tanana answered the knock at her door and looked relieved to discover it was Caroline. The baby cried pitifully in the background.

"Carl cried all night. I think he's sick."

Caroline didn't bother to take off her parka, but walked directly to the baby's side. Gently, she lifted him from the crib bed. His little face was red and his legs were drawn up against his stomach.

"He might have colic."

"Colic?" Tanana repeated.

"Does he cry after each feeding?"

"And before. All he does is cry."

From the Indian girl's obvious exhaustion, Caroline could believe it. "Then I think you should make an appointment with the medical team for next week."

Tanana agreed with a short nod.

"Lie down for a bit and rest," Caroline said softly. "I'll hold Carl."

"You spoil him."

Caroline grinned and kissed the top of his small head. "I know, but let me."

"You'll make a good mother for Paul Trevor's sons."

Some of the light faded from Caroline's eyes and she quickly averted her face so her friend couldn't read her distress. She spent most of the afternoon with Tanana and the baby, leaving only when she was certain that Carl would sleep and that his mother had received a few hours' rest.

"Send Thomas if you need me," she instructed on her way out the door.

Paul met Caroline halfway back to the cabin. His eyes held hers in a long, steady look. "I'll be leaving in a few minutes."

"Would my master wish me to carry his bags to the airstrip?"

"Caroline . . . don't, please."

Keeping up this charade was hard enough when her heart was breaking. "Carl has colic and poor Tanana's been up two nights with him." She tried to cover the uncomfortable silence.

Paul's eyes caressed her. "You don't need to go to the airstrip."

She lowered her gaze, already feeling herself weaken.

Walter met them and loaded Paul's suitcase onto the back of the dogsled. He seemed to realize that Paul and Caroline needed time alone.

"Caroline," he began. This was hard for him, harder than he thought. "You're not a prisoner." He turned her into his arms and held her close, shutting his eyes to savor the feel of her against him. Their coats were so thick that it made holding each other awkward and he reluctantly dropped his arms.

Caroline swallowed her anger. "How long will you be away?"

"Four, possibly five days."

It seemed a lifetime, but she said nothing. His hands caressed her face with such tenderness that Caroline closed her eyes and against every dictate of her will, she swayed toward him. When he fit his mouth over hers, her lips parted with eager welcome. The kiss was long and thorough, making her all the more aware of the seductive power he held over her senses. Of their own volition, her arms slid upward over his chest and around his neck. One kiss and he dominated her will, destroying her weak resolve. Caroline didn't know whom she was more furious with, herself or Paul.

"Oh, love," he breathed against her lips. "Next time maybe you'll come with me."

Purposefully, she stepped away from him. She was irate, frustrated with herself for being so weak and more so with Paul for not trusting her. "I'll be happy to go with you if I'm still here."

The shock that contorted Paul's features and narrowed his eyes caused Caroline to suck in her breath. Abruptly he turned away and left her, marching to the airstrip without a word of farewell.

Caroline didn't know what had made her say anything so incredibly stupid. She regretted her sharp tongue, but Paul had hurt her and she wanted him to realize she wasn't a lifeless rag doll with no feelings.

"Damn!" She stomped her foot in the dry snow. If she'd hoped to build a foundation of trust, she'd just crumpled its cornerstone.

Caroline stood as she was until Paul's plane had taxied away and ascended into the gray sky. Only then did she return to the cabin, disillusioned and miserable. It astonished her how empty the place felt. She remained standing in the middle of the living room for several minutes, hardly able to believe that in the span of a few hours, her entire world could have been jolted so sharply.

That night, Caroline slept fitfully. She was too cold, then too hot. Her pillow was too flat and the mattress sagged on one side. After midnight, she admitted that it wasn't the bed or too many blankets. The problem was that the space beside her was empty. With a sigh, she turned and stared at the ceiling, trying to come up with ways of repairing her marriage.

Paul set his suitcase on the carpeted floor of the Hotel Fairbanks. His room was adequate—a double bed, dresser, chair and television. He stared at the TV set and experienced a small twinge of regret. The sensation multiplied when his gaze fell on the bathtub.

Regret hounded him. Not once in all the weeks that Caroline had been in Atta had she complained about the less-than-ideal living conditions. Yet she'd been denied the most simple of pleasures.

Slowly, Paul removed his parka and carelessly tossed it on top of the bed. He ran his hand over his eyes; he was determined to rush this trip and get back to Caroline and rebuild what his jealous doubts had destroyed.

After he'd undressed and climbed into the soft bed, Paul lay on his back, his arms folded behind his head. It didn't feel right to be here without Caroline. A smile lifted the corners of his mouth as he recalled how quickly she'd dropped her role of servant; she had too much fire in her to play the part with any conviction.

He thought about her being alone in the cabin, curled up and sleeping in his bed, and experienced such an overwhelming surge of desire that his body tightened and tension knotted his stomach. She often slept in that thin fur-lined piece of silk her aunts had given her. Usually it rode up her slim body so that if he reached for her, his hand was met with warm, silken skin.

Paul inhaled sharply at the memory. Her eagerness for his lovemaking had been a surprise and a delight. She hadn't refused him once, welcoming his ardor with an energy and enthusiasm he hadn't hoped to expect. He wouldn't leave her again, wouldn't take another trip unless she could join him. He planned on telling her so the minute he returned to Atta.

Caroline woke early the next morning. As usual it was dark. The hours of daylight were becoming shorter and shorter as they approached the autumnal equinox. More and more of each day was spent in complete darkness. She thought about the summer and what it would be like to have the sun shine late at night. Then she wondered if she'd be in Atta to see it. The thought stunned her. Of course, she'd be in Atta. This was her home now.

No sooner had she dressed and fixed breakfast than there was a knock on her door. Walter Thundercloud stood on the other side, grinning wryly.

"Good morning, Walter."

He nodded politely, stepped inside and looked a bit uneasy.

Without asking, she poured him a cup of coffee and placed it on the table.

"You okay?" he asked gruffly.

"Of course I am."

"Paul asked me to check on you."

Caroline pulled out a chair and sat across from the old Indian. Naturally Paul would want to be sure his prisoner was in her cell. Her hands surrounded the thick mug. "I'm fine. You needn't worry about me."

Walter hesitated. "Paul has been in Atta several years now."

It seemed that her husband's friend was leading up to something. She nodded, hoping that was encouragement enough for him to continue.

"When he first came, he had the cabin built for privacy. The oil company had supplied his quarters, but he wanted something larger and more homelike so he could bring his wife to live with him."

"His wife!" Caroline nearly choked on her coffee. It scalded the inside of her mouth and burned a path all the way to her stomach.

"The woman wasn't his wife yet. She'd only promised to be."

"I see." Paul had been engaged! "What happened?"

"He never told me, but one day a letter arrived and after he read it, Paul left the station and got sick drunk. He never mentioned her name again."

Nor had he mentioned the woman to Caroline. The heat of jealous anger blossomed in her cheeks. The night of her arrival, she'd spilled her guts about Larry. Apparently, Paul had gone through a similar experience and hadn't thought to mention it to her. Talk about trust!

"For many months, Paul was angry. He worked too hard, some nights not sleeping. He scowled and barked and drank more than he should."

"He didn't leave Atta and try to work things out with this woman?"

"No."

Caroline took another sip of her coffee, not surprised. He had an overabundance of pride, oftentimes to his own detriment. "Why are you telling me this?"

"For the first time since Paul Trevor arrived in Atta, he smiles every day. He laughs. Before my eyes I've seen happiness fill him. These changes come when you come.''

So Walter wanted to reassure her. She smiled softly and diverted her attention to her drink, not wanting him to know his words only proved how little she knew of the man who was her husband.

''What made Paul decide to marry now after all this time?''

Walter shrugged. ''I think Tanana had something to do with that.''

''Tanana?'' Caroline didn't understand.

''He wants a family.''

She nodded. Tanana had told her the same thing.

''He loves you,'' Walter continued. ''I don't believe Paul ever thought he'd be fortunate enough to find such a good woman as you. He put the ad in the paper because he was lonely.''

''But why did he advertise for a wife? Surely there were women who would want to marry him. Someone in Fairbanks?''

Walter added sugar to his coffee, stirring it a long time, far longer than necessary. ''You'll have to ask him that.''

Alarm turned her blood cold. ''He has a woman in Fairbanks?''

Walter chuckled and shook his head. ''Not as far as I know. He advertised for a woman because he hadn't the time to properly date someone and build a relationship by the usual means. Then, too, I think he feared the same thing would happen to him a second time and she would change her mind.''

No wonder he'd been so insistent that they stayed married. "Why is a child so important to Paul?"

"I don't know. I suppose it was because he never had a family himself."

This was another shock to Caroline. Paul had spoken only briefly about his background. He'd been raised somewhere in Texas. As far as she knew, he hadn't contacted his parents about their marriage and now that she thought about it, Paul seemed to change the subject whenever she mentioned anything about his childhood.

The faded eyes brightened. "I'm not telling you these things to stir up trouble." The old man paused and chuckled. "I can see that most of what I've said has been a shock. I don't know that Paul would appreciate my loose tongue, but I felt you should know that he's gone through some hard times. You've been damn good for that boy."

"Our relationship is still on rocky ground."

"I can see that. I was surprised he didn't take you to Fairbanks and when I mentioned it, he nearly bit my head off."

"You were right when you guessed that I love him."

"He's equally smitten. He'd move heaven and earth to see that you were happy. He may have married just so he could have a son, but he loves you."

Another knock sounded, drawing their attention to the front door. Thomas Eagleclaw stepped in without waiting for an invitation. His eyes were round and eager. "Mrs. Paul, please hurry come."

"What is it?"

"Tanana and baby sick."

An exchange of the native tongue flew over Caroline's head as she stood and reached for her coat. Momentarily, her gaze collided with Walter's. The older man reached for his parka as well and followed her to the Eagleclaws' cabin. Even before they reached the small log structure, Caroline had a premonition of disaster. Her chest tightened with dread.

The baby lay in his bed, hardly moving. His round eyes looked up at her and when Caroline felt his skin, he was burning up with fever. "How long has he been like this?"

"Apparently Tanana's been ill as well." Walter answered for the young man.

"Why didn't you come and get me?" Caroline asked Thomas.

"Tanana probably told him not to; she didn't want to trouble you," Walter whispered, standing close at Caroline's side.

"But Carl is very sick."

"Mary Finefeather has fever," Thomas announced.

"Mary, too?"

Caroline turned to Walter. "I'll do what I can here and meet you at Mary's."

Walter nodded, and left.

Tanana's young face felt hot, and the girl whimpered softly when Caroline tried to talk to her.

The young husband stood stiffly by the bedside. "She's much worse this morning."

"Oh, Thomas, I wish you'd come for me," Caroline said, more sharply than she intended.

The young man looked guiltily at the floor.

"How are you feeling?"

He shrugged, still not looking at her.

Caroline pressed the back of her hand to his forehead and shook her head. "Get in bed and I'll be back when I can."

Although she tried to be calm, her heart was racing. She hurried from the Eagleclaws' to Mary's cabin on the other side of the village. Once there, Caroline discovered that the older woman's symptoms were similar to Tanana's and the baby's.

"Walter, contact the Public Health Department and see if they can fly in some help. I don't know what we've got here, but I don't like the looks of it."

Walter's eyes met her own, dark and serious. "In the winter of 1979 we lost twelve to the fever."

"We're not going to lose anyone. Now get on the wire and hurry!"

Paul paused on the sidewalk outside the jewelry store to look at the diamond rings on display. He'd never thought to ask Caroline if she wanted a diamond. She wore the simple gold band he'd given her and hadn't asked for anything more. Now he wondered if she was disappointed with the simplicity of the ring.

He thought about the gifts he'd already purchased her and realized he'd probably need to buy another suitcase to haul them all back to Atta. He smiled at the thought. He'd bought her everything she'd ever mentioned wanting and, in addition, purchased gifts for Tanana and the baby, knowing Caroline had wanted something special for the two. In his own way, Paul longed to make up to her for excluding her from this trip. Never again would he leave her behind. He decided he'd buy her a ring and save it for Christmas. Everything else he'd give her when he arrived home.

Never had he been more anxious to return to Atta.

The Public Health Department flew in a doctor and two nurses the same afternoon that Walter contacted them. The community meeting hall served as a makeshift hospital and the worst of the sick were brought there. Tanana, the baby and Mary Finefeather were the first to become seriously ill. Others soon followed. Within two days, Caroline and the medical staff tended twenty-five patients. The following day it was thirty, then thirty-five.

"How long has it been since you slept?" Dr. Mather asked Caroline on the third day.

Her smile was weak. "I forget."

"That's what I thought. Go rest, and that's an order."

She stiffened her back and shook her head. She couldn't leave when so many were sick and more arrived every hour. The other staff members had rested intermittently. "I'm fine."

"If you don't do as I say, you'll be sick next."

"I'm not leaving."

"Stubborn woman." But his eyes spoke of admiration and appreciation.

Later the same day, Walter brought her something to eat and forced her to sit down. "I think I should contact Paul."

"Don't." She placed her hand on his forearm and silently pleaded with him. "He'd only worry."

"I think he should. You're working yourself into an early grave."

"I'm as healthy as an ox."

"You won't be if you continue like this."

Walter gave her one of his looks and Caroline slowly shook her head. "All right, we'll compromise. I'll go lie down in a few minutes, but I'll have someone wake me after an hour."

Mary Finefeather died early the next morning. Caroline stood at Dr. Mather's side as he pulled the sheet over the proud Indian face, relaxed now in death. Tears burned the backs of Caroline's eyes, but she dared not let them flow. So many needed her; she had to be strong.

"Are you okay?" the doctor asked.

"I think so," Caroline answered in a strangled voice. "What about the baby?" She'd held Carl for most of the night. He was so weak, too weak to cry. He had lain limp in her arms, barely moving.

The doctor hesitated. "It doesn't look good. If he lasts through the day, then his chances will improve."

The floor pitched beneath her feet. She'd known it herself, but had been afraid to admit it. "His mother?"

"She's young and strong. She should make it."

"Anyone else?"

"Two others look serious."

Caroline bit the soft flesh inside her cheek and followed him to the bed of the next patient.

At the end of the fourth day, Paul returned to the hotel, packed his bags, and checked out. He felt as anxious as a kid awaiting the end of the school term. He was going home to Atta, home to Caroline—his wife, his love. After a short trip to a pizza parlor, the taxi delivered him at the airport. If Burt Manners was late, Paul swore he'd have his hide.

The pilot was waiting for Paul at the designated area inside the terminal. Burt rose to his feet as Paul approached him.

"I've got bad news for you," he said, frowning as he eyed the pizza box.

"What's that?"

"We aren't going to be able to fly into Atta."

"Why the hell not?" Frustration caused Paul to tighten his grip around the handle of his suitcase.

"A white-out."

"Damn!" Paul expelled the word viciously. A white-out was dangerous enough to put the finest, most experienced pilot on edge. Visibility plummeted to zero, making a thick London fog preferable. The condition could last for days.

"There's nothing more you can do." Dr. Mather spoke gently to Caroline and attempted to remove the lifeless four-year-old child from her arms.

"No, please," she whispered, bringing the still body closer to her own. "Let me hold her a few minutes longer. I . . . I just want to say goodbye."

The doctor stepped aside and waited.

Caroline brushed the thick hair from the sweet face and kissed the smooth brow, rocking her gently to and fro in her arms, singing the little girl a lullaby she would never hear. Anna was dead and Caroline was sure Carl was next. Tears rained unchecked down her cheeks. She took a moment to compose herself, then handed the child to the doctor. "I'll tell her mother."

A week after Paul had left Atta, he returned. Walter Thundercloud was at the airstrip waiting for him when the plane taxied to a standstill. One look at the deep, troubled frown and sad eyes that marred the Indian's features and Paul knew that something was terribly wrong.

"What is it?"

"The fever came. Five are dead."

Fear tightened Paul's throat. "Caroline?"

"She's been working for three days without sleep. Thank God, you're back."

"Take me to her."

By the time Paul reached the meeting hall, his heart was pounding. Rarely had he moved more quickly. If anything happened to Caroline, he'd blame himself. He'd left her, abandoned her to some unspeakable fate. He stopped in the doorway, appalled at the scene. The stench hit him first; the hall smelled like death. Stretchers littered the floor, children were crying.

It took him a moment to find Caroline. She was bent over an old woman, lifting the weary head and helping her to sip liquid through a straw. Caroline looked frail and fragile and when she straightened, she staggered and nearly fell backward.

Paul was at her side instantly. She turned and looked at him as though he were a stranger.

"I'm getting you out of here," Paul said, furious that she'd worked herself into this condition and no one had stopped her.

"No, please," she said in a voice so weak it wobbled. "I'm fine." With that, she promptly fainted.

Paul caught her before she hit the floor.

Chapter Nine

Caroline struggled to open her eyes; the lids felt incredibly heavy. She discovered Paul sleeping awkwardly in a kitchen chair at her bedside. He was slouched so that his head rested against the back. One arm hugged his ribs and the other hung loosely at his side. Caroline blinked. Paul looked terrible; his clothes were wrinkled and disorderly, his shirt was pulled out from the waistband and half-unbuttoned.

"Paul?" she whispered, having difficulty finding her voice. She forced herself to swallow. When Paul didn't respond, Caroline lifted her hand and tugged at his shirttail.

His eyes flew open instantly and he bolted upright. "Caroline? Oh God, you're awake." He rose to his feet and brushed his unkempt hair from his face, staring down at her as if he couldn't quite believe it was she. "How do you feel?"

The past week suddenly returned to haunt her in technicolor detail. She thought of Mary Finefeather and her abrupt one-word sentences and Anna, the bubbly four-year-old. An overwhelming sadness at the loss of her friends brought stinging tears to her eyes.

"Carl?" She managed to squeeze the name of the baby from the tightness that claimed her throat.

"He's improving and so is Tanana."

"Good." Caroline closed her eyes again because sleep was preferable to the memories.

When she awakened a second time, Paul was sitting in the chair beside their bed. Only this time his head was slouched forward, his elbows resting on his knees, his face buried in his hands. She must have made a sound; he slowly lifted his head.

"How long have I been asleep?" she asked.

"Forty-eight hours."

She arched her eyebrows in surprise. "Did I catch the fever?"

"The doctor said it was exhaustion." Paul stood and poured a glass of water and lifted her head so she could sip from it. When she'd finished, he gently lowered her back to the bed.

Caroline rolled her face away so she wouldn't have to watch his expression. "I want to go home."

"Caroline, love, you are home."

Her eyes drifted closed. She hadn't thought it would be easy; she knew Paul too well.

"Caroline, I know you're upset, but you'll feel different later. I promise you will."

Despite her resolve not to cry, a tear coursed down her cheek. "I hate Alaska. I want to go where death doesn't come with the dark, where children laugh and I can smell flowers again." People had died here— people she had loved, people she had cared about. Friends. Children. Babies. The marriage she'd worked so hard to build wasn't a real one. The only ingredient that held it together was Paul's indomitable pride; he wasn't going to let her go after he'd already lost one woman.

"You don't know what you're saying," he stated, discounting her words as he reached for her hand.

"I want to go home."

"Caroline! Damn it!" He released her hand and she heard him stalk to the other side of the room. "I'll fix you something to eat."

Alone now, Caroline pushed back the covers and carefully sat upright. The room spun and teetered, but she gripped the headboard and gradually everything righted itself.

Suddenly she felt terribly hungry. When Paul returned, carrying a tray of tea, toast and scrambled eggs, she gave no thought to refusing it.

He fluffed up her pillows against the headboard and set the tray on her lap. It looked as though he meant to feed her, and Caroline stopped him with her hand.

"I can do it."

He nodded and sat back in the chair. "Walter said you nearly killed yourself. You refused to leave, or rest or eat. Why did you push yourself like that, love?" He paused and watched her lift the fork to her mouth with unhurried, deliberate movements. "He told me about Anna dying in your arms."

Caroline chewed slowly, but not by choice; even eating required energy. She didn't want to talk about Anna, the fever, or anything else. She didn't answer Paul's questions because she couldn't explain to him something that she didn't fully understand herself. In some incomprehensible way, she felt responsible for the people in Atta. They were her friends, her family, and she'd let them down.

"I can't tell you how bad I feel that you were left to deal..."

"Why didn't you mention her?"

Paul gave her an odd look. "Mention who?"

She glared at him. "You know *who*."

"Oh Lord, don't tell me we're going to go through this again. Should I wear padded clothes as protection against the salt and pepper shakers?" Mockingly he held up his hands, his eyes twinkling.

For a moment, Caroline was furious enough to hurl something at him, but it required more energy than she was willing to expend.

"Caroline, love..."

"I'm not your love," she said heatedly.

Paul chuckled. "You can't honestly mean that after the last few weeks."

"Correction," she said bitterly. "I'm not your *first* love."

Paul went still and his eyes narrowed. "All right, what did you find?"

"Find?" Caroline discovered she was shaking. "Find? Do you mean to tell me that you've got . . . memorabilia stored in this cabin from that . . . that other woman?''

''Caroline, settle down . . .''

''Oh-h-h.'' It required all her restraint not to fling a leftover piece of toast at him. He must have noticed her temptation because he quickly lifted the tray from her lap and returned it to the kitchen.

While he was gone, Caroline lay back down and tried to compose her thoughts. He'd loved another woman so much that it had taken years for him to commit himself to a new relationship. Caroline was simply filling some other woman's place in his life. What bothered her most was that he'd never mentioned a previous lover. The more she learned, the more imperative it became for her to leave.

He returned to the bedroom, his steps reluctant, almost hesitant. The tips of his fingers were slipped into the back pockets of his jeans. ''This isn't the time to talk about Diane. When you're stronger, I'll tell you everything you want to know.''

''Diane,'' Caroline repeated slowly, and vowed to hate every woman with that name. An eerie calm came over her as she suspiciously raised her eyes to meet Paul's. ''This . . . Diane didn't happen to be blond, blue-eyed, about five-five and have an hourglass figure, did she?''

Paul looked stunned. ''You knew her?''

''You idiot, that's me!'' She grabbed a pillow from his side of the bed and heaved it at him with all her strength. She was so weak that it didn't even make it to the end of the mattress.

Innocently, Paul raised both his hands. "Love, listen, I know what this sounds like."

"Get out!"

"Caroline."

"No doubt the doctor told you I should remain calm and quiet. The very sight of you boils my blood, Paul Trevor, so kindly leave before there's cardiovascular damage!"

He advanced toward her and Caroline scrambled to her knees and reached for the glass of water. "You take one more step and you'll be wearing this!"

Exasperated, Paul swore under his breath. "How one woman could be so utterly unreasonable is beyond me."

"Unreasonable!" She lifted the tumbler and brought back her arm, making the threat more real. The action was enough to force him to exit the room. Once he'd gone, Caroline curled up in a tight ball and shook with fury and shock. Not only hadn't he told her about Diane, but he'd chosen Caroline because she obviously resembled the other woman. He'd told her often enough that one look at her picture and he'd known. Sure he'd known! She was a duplicate of the woman he'd once loved.... And probably still did.

Blissfully, Caroline escaped into a deep slumber. When she awakened, she felt stronger and, although she was a bit shaky on her feet, she managed to dress and pull out the suitcase from beneath the bed. Her hands trembled as she neatly folded and packed each garment.

"What are you doing?" Paul asked from behind her.

Caroline stiffened. "What I should have done weeks ago. Leaving Atta. Leaving Alaska. Leaving you."

"I won't let you, love," he said after a long, tension-wrought moment. "I realize things are a bit unsettled between us, but we'll work it out."

"Unsettled. You call this unsettled? Well, I've got news for you, Paul Trevor. Things are a little more than just unsettled. I want out. O-U-T. Out!"

"There will be no divorce."

"Fine, we'll stay married if that's what you want. We'll have the ideal marriage—I'll be in Seattle and you can live here. No more arguing. No more disagreements. No more Scrabble." Frantically, she stacked her sweaters in the open suitcase. "Believe me, after this experience I don't wish to involve myself with another man again."

"Caroline..."

"I'll tell you one thing I'm grateful for, though," she interrupted him; talking helped to relieve the terrible ache in her breast. "You taught me a lot about myself. Here I was playing Joan of Arc to an entire Indian village as if I were some heroic soul. I was a real Clara Barton dispensing medical knowledge and good will with the best of them."

"Caroline..."

"I even fooled myself into thinking you and I could make a go of this marriage. I thought, 'Gee, Paul Trevor's a good man. Better than most. Fair. Kind. Tender.' I'll admit that the events leading up to our marriage were a bit bizarre, but I was ready to stick it out and make the most of the situation. Things could have been worse—I could have married Larry." She laughed then, but the sound contained little amusement.

His hands settled on her shoulders and he attempted to turn her around, but Caroline wouldn't let him. "Please, don't touch me." He was warm and gentle and she couldn't resist him. Her eyes filled with tears and Paul swam in and out of her vision as she backed away from him.

"I can't let you go, love," he said softly.

"You don't have any choice."

"Caroline, give it a week. You're distraught now, but in a few days, you'll feel differently."

"No," she sobbed, jerking her head back and forth. "I can't stay another day. Please, I need to get away."

"Let me hold you for just a minute."

"No." But she didn't fight him when he reached for her and brought her into the warm circle of his arms.

"I know, love," he whispered, and felt his heart catch at the anguish in her tormented features. She buried her face in his shirt and wept, her shoulders shaking with such force that Paul braced his feet to hold her securely.

"She died in my arms," she wailed.

"I know, love, I know." His hand smoothed her hair in long, even strokes. Regret sliced though him like a hot knife. He'd left her to face this alone, never dreaming anything like a fever could happen, thinking only of himself. He'd been incredibly selfish.

When her tears were spent, Caroline raised her head and wiped the moisture from her face. Paul's shirt bore evidence of her crying and she guiltily tried to rub away the wet stains.

His hand stopped hers and tenderly raised her palm to his mouth. He kissed the inside of her hand while his eyes held hers. She didn't want him to be so gentle; she wanted to hate him so she could leave and never look back.

"Please, don't," she pleaded weakly.

Paul released her hand.

"Caroline," he said seriously. "I can't let you go."

"Why not? Nothing binds us except a thin piece of paper." He flinched at her words and she regretted hurting him.

"I love you."

Knotting her hands into fists, she raised her chin a fraction. "Did you love Diane, too?"

Paul's face seemed to lose its color.

"Did you?" she cried, her voice raised.

"Yes."

Caroline pressed her advantage. "You let her go. You didn't go after her and force her to marry you and live on this frozen chunk of ice. I'm only asking for the same consideration."

"You don't know..."

"I do. I know everything there is about Alaska and Atta. I know that I can't live here anymore. I know I can't look you in the face and feel I'm your wife and you're my husband. I know I can't bear any more pain. Please, Paul, let me go home." She was weeping again, almost uncontrollably.

Paul advanced a step toward her. "You'll feel better tomorrow," he said softly, then turned and left the room.

Caroline slumped on top of the bed and cried until her eyes burned and there were no more tears. Spent, she slept again, only to awaken in a dark, shadowless room. Someone, probably Paul, had placed a thick blanket over her shoulders. She sat up and brushed the unruly mass of hair from her face.

Instantly, Paul stood in the doorway. "You're awake."

"Yes, master."

He sighed, but said nothing more.

"I've fixed you something to eat. Would you like to come out here or would you rather I brought it in to you?"

"Whatever my master wishes."

He clenched his fists. "It'll be on the table when you're ready."

"Thank you, master." Her words were spoken in a monotone.

Patience, Paul told himself. That was the key. Caroline had been through a traumatic experience that had mentally and physically exhausted her. She needed to know she was loved and that he would be there to protect her against anything like this happening again. For the hundredth time, he cursed himself for having left her while he'd gallivanted off to Fairbanks.

He ladled out a bowl of rich vegetable soup and set it on the table along with thick slices of sourdough bread. Next he poured her a tall glass of milk.

Caroline changed clothes and brushed her teeth and hair. She looked a sight; it was a wonder Paul wasn't happy to be rid of her.

Paul glanced up expectantly when she entered the room and pulled out a kitchen chair for her to sit down. Unfolding the napkin, Caroline spread it across her lap and stared at the meal. Although it smelled delicious, she had no appetite.

Her lack of interest must have shown in her eyes because Paul spoke sharply. "Eat, Caroline."

"I . . . I don't think I can."

"Try."

"I want to go home."

Paul's fists were so tight his fingers ached. *Patience,* he reminded himself for the tenth time, and she'd only been awake a few hours.

He took the chair across from her, straddled it and watched her as she methodically lifted the spoon to her mouth. "I brought you something from Fairbanks. Would you like to see it?" he coaxed.

She tried to smile, but there was nothing left of her strength. All she could think about was Seattle and her two aunts and how the world seemed to be right there. There was too much pain in Atta. "Will you let me go home if I look at it?"

A muscle leapt in his temple, but he refused to rise to the bait. He stood, opened the closet door and brought her several packages.

"Go ahead and open them," he said eagerly, then changed his mind. "No. You eat, I'll open them for you." From the first package, he produced an expensive bottle of perfume she'd once mentioned enjoying. He glanced expectantly to her, anticipating her delight.

Caroline swallowed down her surprise. He could be so loving and she didn't want him to be. Not now when all she could think about was leaving him.

"Well?"

"It's very nice. Thank you, master."

Paul had had it. His fist slammed down on the table and he shot to his feet. "You will never call me your master again. Is that understood?"

"Yes."

"I wish you'd stop this silly game!"

"Will you let me go home if I do?" Caroline asked and took another spoonful of soup.

Paul ignored the question and from the second package withdrew a huge teddy bear and was pleased when she paused, the spoon lifted halfway to her mouth.

"For Carl," he explained. "You said you wanted something special for him. I thought we'd save it for Christmas."

She nodded, and recalled how close they'd come to losing the baby. Tears filled her eyes.

Paul turned the bear over and ran his hand through the thick fur. "You twist something in the back here and Mr. Bear actually talks."

Caroline's nod was nearly imperceptible.

"Would you like to see what I got Tanana?"

"Not now . . . please." She looked straight ahead, and felt dizzy and weak. Setting the spoon back on the table she closed her eyes. "Would it be all right if I lay down a minute?"

"Of course." He moved to her side and slipped an arm around her waist as he guided her back into the bedroom. The suitcase was open on top of the bed. Paul moved it and set it on top of the dresser.

Caroline felt listless and tired. "Do I really look so much like her?"

"Her? You mean Diane?"

Caroline nodded.

"Now that you mention it, I suppose there's a certain resemblance, but it's only superficial."

"Why didn't you tell me about her?"

"It's a long story. Too complicated for right now."

"And you think my involvement with Larry wasn't?"

Paul sighed and closed the lid of her suitcase. "The two aren't comparable."

"What about your family?"

Paul went tense. "Who mentioned that?"

"We're married," she said sadly, "and yet you hide your life from me."

"I have no family, love. I was raised in a series of foster homes."

"You tell me about your childhood, but not Diane. I think I know the reasons why."

Irritated, Paul shook his head, his mouth pinched and white. "I love you."

"Then let me go back to Seattle," she pleaded.

"No, now don't ask me that again."

"Yes, master."

Paul groaned and slammed the door.

If Paul thought Caroline would give up her quest to return to Seattle, he was wrong. For two days, she sat around the cabin, listless and lethargic, staring into space. She never spoke unless spoken to and answered his questions with as few words as possible. She wore her unhappiness like an oversized cloak that smothered her natural exuberance.

He tried to draw her out, tried reasoning with her. Nothing helped. By the time they climbed into bed at night, he was so frustrated with her that any desire for lovemaking was destroyed. He longed to hold her, yearned to feel her body close to his, but each time he reached for her, she froze up.

She didn't mention returning to Seattle again. She didn't have to; the misery was evident in her eyes. Her suitcase remained packed and ready, a constant reminder of how eager she was to leave him. He placed it back under the bed once, but she immediately withdrew it and set it by the front door, waiting for him to release her. He let her keep the suitcase there because she'd only put it back if he moved it. He couldn't let her leave Atta; he couldn't lose her.

Each morning Paul promised himself Caroline would be better, but she tried his patience to the breaking point. He had to find a way to reach her and was quickly running out of ideas.

But today, he vowed, would be different. He had a plan.

After dinner that evening, Paul sat in his recliner, reading the Fairbanks newspaper. His mind whirled with thoughts of seduction; he missed Caroline; he missed having the warm, loving woman in his arms. It had been nearly two weeks since they'd made love and if anything could shatter the barriers she'd built against him, it was their lovemaking. He smiled, content for the first time in days.

"Caroline."

She turned to him, her eyes blank. "Yes."

"Dinner was very good tonight."

"Thank you."

"Would you come here a minute, please?"

She stepped toward him in small, measured steps, refusing to meet his eyes, and paused directly in front of the recliner.

"Sit on my lap."

Caroline hesitated, but did as he requested.

His hand massaged her tense muscles. "Relax," he whispered.

Caroline found it impossible to do so, but said nothing.

"Okay, love, place your hands on my shoulders."

She did that, too, with a fair amount of reluctance.

"Now kiss me."

Her eyes narrowed as she recognized his game.

"You're so fond of calling me your master, I thought you might need a little direction."

She didn't move.

"Just one kiss, love?"

Lightly, she rested the heels of her hands on his shoulders and leaned forward.

"Okay, love, kiss me."

Caroline stared at him blankly and gently pressed her closed mouth over his.

"No, love, a *real* kiss. One that will turn my socks inside out."

Caroline rubbed her closed mouth over his in the briefest of contacts.

"I've never known you to be so selfish. It'll be Christmas soon, and even a grinch could do better than that."

With the tip of her tongue, she moistened her lips and slanted her head to press her mouth over his. She felt like this was all a dream and it wasn't really happening.

The kiss was routine. Paul wove her hair around his fingers and placed his hand at the back of her head, holding her to him. His warmth permeated her heart and Caroline felt herself soften.

"I've missed your kisses, love." His eyes held hers. "I've missed everything about you."

Caroline couldn't seem to tear her gaze from his.

"Kiss me again—oh, love, you taste so good."

He tasted wonderful too, and Caroline settled her mouth over his, her lips parted enough so that she couldn't protest. With a sigh, she surrendered, admitting defeat.

Before she even realized what had happened, Paul had removed her blouse and was lazily running his hands over her bare breasts, praising her, telling her again and again how much he loved her.

He continued to kiss her with an urgency that quickly became an all-consuming passion. She felt weak, spent. Her arms clung to Paul and when he ran his hand along the inside of her thigh, she squirmed, wanting more and more of him. Her fingers shook almost uncontrollably as she pulled the shirt tail from his waist band and rubbed her palms over his chest.

"Oh Lord, love, I want you."

Somehow those words permeated the fog of desire when the others hadn't. With a soft moan, she lifted her head from his and stared at him with tear-filled eyes.

"Love?" He reached for her and she moved away as though he held a gun in his hand.

"Paul, please, I can't live here anymore. It hurts too much. Forcing me to stay only makes it worse."

His face lost all color. He could see it would do no good to reason with her, and sighed with defeat. "Alaska is my home."

"But it isn't mine."

"You'll get over this," he promised gently.

"I can't . . . I won't. I tried, Paul, I honestly tried."

He was silent for so long that Caroline wondered if he was going to speak again. "I won't come after you, Caroline. I didn't for Diane and I won't for you."

She nodded numbly. "I understand."

His fists bunched at his side. "I won't keep you against your will any longer."

Tears streaked her face and when she spoke, her voice was low and rusty. "Thank you."

"Shall I arrange for the divorce or would you rather do it yourself?"

Chapter Ten

Oh, Sister," Ethel Myers said with a worried frown, "I don't know that the brew will help dear Caroline this time."

"We must think, and you know as well as I do that we do it so much better with Father's brew." With exaggerated movements, Mabel Myers poured two steaming cups of the spiked tea and handed one to her younger sister.

"Poor Caroline."

Mabel placed the dainty cup to her lips, paused and sighed. "She sounded so happy in her letters."

"And she tries so hard to hide her unhappiness now."

"Paul Trevor must be a terrible beast to have treated her so..."

"He isn't, Aunt Mabel," Caroline said from the archway of her aunts' parlor. "He's a wonderful man. Good and kind. Generous and unselfish."

Ethel reached for another porcelain cup. "Tea, dear?"

"Not me," Caroline said with a grin, recalling the last time she'd sampled her great-grandfather's brew. Before she'd known what was happening, she'd been married to Paul Trevor and was lying in his bed.

"If he wasn't a beast, dear, then why did you leave him?"

Caroline claimed a seat on the thick brocade sofa and sadly shook her head. "For silly reasons, I suppose."

"Silly reasons?" Ethel echoed, and the two older women exchanged meaningful glances.

"Then, dear, perhaps you should go back."

Caroline dropped her gaze to her lap. "I can't."

"Can't?" Mabel repeated. "Why ever not?"

"There was another woman. . . ."

"With him?" Ethel sounded shocked. "Why, that's indecent. He *is* a beast."

"He loved Diane a long time ago," Caroline corrected hurriedly. "He never told me about her, but when he gave me the ticket home, he said that he didn't go after Diane and he wasn't coming after me."

Mabel placed her hand on top of Caroline's and squeezed gently. "Do you love him, dear?"

Caroline nodded. "Very much."

"Then you must go to him."

Her two aunts made it all sound so easy. Every day since she'd been home, Caroline had thought of Paul.

He'd been right. Time had healed her from the shock of losing her friends to the fever. She'd been distraught; the people who had died hadn't been nameless faces in sterile hospital beds, but friends. They had been a part of her Alaskan family and each one had touched her heart in a special way.

"Go to him?" Caroline repeated and sadly shook her head. "No."

"No?" both sisters exclaimed together.

"If he loved me enough, he'd come to me. I need that, although I don't expect anyone else to understand the reasons why."

The doorbell chimed and Caroline stood. "That must be Larry. We're going to a movie."

"Have a good time, dear."

"Oh yes, dear, have a good time."

No sooner had the front door closed than Ethel glanced at her sister, her eyes twinkling with mischief. "Shall I get the stationery or will you?"

"Hi." Larry kissed Caroline lightly on the forehead. "At least you've got some color in your face tonight."

"Thank you," she said, and laughed. Leave it to Larry to remind her that she'd been pale and sickly for four weeks. "And you're looking dashing, as usual." It nearly frightened her now to think that they'd almost married. Larry would make someone a wonderful husband, but Caroline wasn't that woman.

"Is there any movie you'd particularly like to see?" he asked.

"You choose." Their tastes were so different that anything she opted for would only be grounds for a lively discussion.

"There's a musical playing at the Fifth Avenue."

His choice surprised Caroline. Musicals weren't his thing. Blood and gore were what thrilled Larry.

"Do you approve?"

Caroline looked up at him and was forced to blink back tears. She hadn't cried since she'd returned to Seattle. Tears were a useless emotion now. She was home and everything was supposed to be roses and sunshine. Only it wasn't, because Paul wasn't there to share it with her. She'd been a fool to leave him and even more of one not to admit her mistake and go back.

"I've said something to upset you?" Larry asked kindly, offering her his handkerchief. It was clean and ironed and so like him that Caroline only wept louder.

"Caroline?"

She blew her nose loudly and handed him back his hanky.

He stared at the wadded mass of white cotton and shook his head. "You go ahead and keep it."

"Paul liked musicals," she explained, and sniffled. "He can't sing worth beans, but he didn't hesitate to belt out a song like Mario Lanza." She paused and giggled. "And then he'd ask: 'Is it live or is it Memorex?'"

"You really dug this guy, didn't you?"

"He was the only man I ever knew who could beat me in a game of Scrabble."

"He beat you in Scrabble?" Even Larry sounded impressed. "As far as I can see, you two were meant for each other. Now when are you going to admit it?"

"Never, I fear," she said and an incredible sadness settled over her.

Ethel Myers sat in front of the antique typewriter and looked thoughtfully toward her sibling. "Pour me another glass of tea, will you, Sister?"

"Most certainly, Sister."

They looked at each other and giggled like schoolgirls.

"Caroline must never know."

"Oh no. Caroline most definitely would not approve."

"Read the letter again, Sister."

Ethel picked up the single sheet of linen paper and sighed. "My darling Paul," she said in a breathless whisper, as though she were a great actress practicing her lines. "I feel you should know that I find myself with child. Your loving wife, Caroline."

"Excellent. Excellent."

"We'll put it in the mail first thing tomorrow."

"More brew, Sister?"

Ethel giggled and held out her cup. "Indeed."

A week later, Caroline lay on the end of her bed and admitted defeat. Paul wasn't coming for her. He'd told her he wouldn't so it shouldn't be any great shock, but she'd hoped he would. If he loved her, truly loved her, then he would have forsaken his pride and come to

Seattle to claim her as his woman. So much for dreams.

She turned onto her side. Surely, he must realize that she was waiting for him. She needed proof of his love—proof that she was more important to him than Diane had ever been. She was his wife, his love. He'd told her so countless times.

A sour taste filled her mouth. Admitting she was wrong wouldn't be easy. Look how long it had taken her to realize how mismatched she and Larry were.

Caroline sighed expressively and closed her eyes. Carl would have his first tooth by now. She missed the baby, and Tanana and the long talks they'd shared. She missed the women of the village and the authentic Indian sweaters she used to knit for the tourists. She missed the dusk at noon and the nonstop snow and even the unrelenting cold.

Most of all she missed Paul. He might have been able to live without her, but she was wilting away for lack of him.

With the realization that Paul's pride would keep him in Alaska came an unpleasant insight; it was up to her to swallow her considerable pride and go to him.

Within twenty minutes, her luggage was packed. She'd waited five weeks and another day was intolerable. She'd go to him. She hated the thought, but her love was too strong to give her peace.

"Are you going someplace, dear?" Aunt Mabel asked as Caroline descended the stairs, a suitcase in each hand.

"Alaska."

"Alaska?" Mabel cried, as though Caroline had suggested outer space.

Immediately Ethel appeared and Mabel cast a stricken gaze toward her sister. "Caroline claims she's going to Alaska!"

"But she can't!" Ethel cried.

"I can't?" Perplexed, Caroline glanced from one addled face to the other. Only last week the pair had suggested she return.

"Oh, dear, this is a problem."

Ethel looked uncomfortable. "Perhaps we should tell her, Sister."

"Perhaps we should."

Caroline knew her lovable aunts well enough to realize they'd been plotting again. "I think you'd better start at the beginning."

Fifteen minutes later, after hearing all the details, Caroline accepted a cup of the brew. She needed it. "Paul will come," she murmured. Never having one of his own, Paul wanted a family.

"He'll come and then you'll be happy. Isn't that right, dear?"

Her aunts gave her a look of such innocence, she couldn't disillusion them. "Right," Caroline said weakly.

"You were going back to him," Ethel pointed out.

"Yes." But this was different. At least if she returned to Atta, Paul would have his pride intact. But now, he would believe he'd been tricked again, and that wouldn't set right with her husband. Her aunts' meddling once was Paul's limit.

"You're not unhappy, are you, dear?" Mabel queried softly.

"I'm happy," she replied. "Very happy." Briefly, she wondered how long she could disguise the fact that she wasn't pregnant.

Her aunts returned the teapot to the kitchen while Caroline remained in the room off the entry that her aunts insisted on calling the parlor. The doorbell gave a musical chime and, still bemused from the tea and her aunts' schemes, Caroline rose to answer it.

The man who stood outside the door was tall and well built. Strong and muscular. Caroline glanced up at him expectantly and blinked, finding him vaguely familiar.

"Caroline, I know..."

"Paul?" She widened her eyes to study him and her mouth dropped open. It was Paul, but without a beard. Good grief, he was handsome! Extraordinarily good-looking! Without realizing what she was doing, she lifted her hand to his clean-shaven face and ran the tips of her fingers over the lean, square jaw.

"May I come in?"

For a moment, Caroline was too flabbergasted to react. "Oh, of course. I'm sorry." Hurriedly, she stepped aside so he could enter the Victorian house, and then led him into the parlor. "Please sit down."

He wore gray slacks, the Irish cable knit sweater she'd made for him and a thin jacket. Everyone else in Seattle was wearing wool coats and mufflers and claiming it was the coldest winter in fifty years.

"How are you, Caroline?"

She was starving for the sight of him and so incredibly pleased that she couldn't take her eyes off his smooth jaw. "Fine," she said absently. Then she remembered what her aunts had told him and frowned. "Actually, I haven't been well, but that's to be expected." She placed her hand on her stomach and hoped she exuded a pregnant look. "How are you?" No doubt the news of her condition had come as a shock.

"Fine."

Having forgotten her manners once, Caroline quickly tried to right her earlier lack of welcome. "Would you like some tea?"

"Coffee, if you have it." He paused and looked at the ornate frames on the mantel that pictured her two aunts and added, "Just plain coffee."

"But you drank your coffee with cream before."

"I meant with cream. It's the other things I'm hoping to avoid."

Her bewilderment must have shown in her eyes. "I don't want any of your aunts' brew."

"Oh, right."

Caroline rushed into the kitchen and returned with a cup of coffee for Paul and a tall glass of milk for herself. He'd insist that she eat right if she were pregnant. Her two aunts joined her and when the small party entered the room, Paul stood.

"You must be Ethel and Mabel," he said politely.

They nodded in unison.

"He's even more handsome in person, don't you think, Sister?"

"Oh, most definitely."

"Caroline," Paul grumbled when the two older women showed no signs of leaving the parlor. "Could we go someplace and talk?"

"Oh, do go, dear," Ethel encouraged with a broad grin.

"Someplace *private*," Mabel whispered, and the way she said it suggested a hotel room. Even Caroline blushed.

Paul escorted her to the car, a rental, she noted, and opened the passenger door for her. She couldn't stop staring at him. He looked so different—compelling, forthright, determined.

Once she was seated inside, he paused and ran his hand over the side of his face. "I feel naked without it."

"Why... why did you shave?"

He gave her an odd look. "For you."

"Me?"

"You once said you refused to stay married to a man when you couldn't see his face."

Caroline remembered his response, too. He'd told her to get used to his beard because it was nature's protection from the Alaskan winter. He'd adamantly refused to shave then, but he'd done it now because this "pretend pregnancy" was so important to him. She should be the happiest woman alive, but unexpectedly Caroline felt like crying.

"I said several things," she answered, her gaze lowered to her clenched hands in her lap. "A lot of them weren't necessarily true." She dreaded telling him there wasn't any baby and wondered how long she could pretend. This was no way to negotiate a reconciliation. "How's Tanana?" she asked, changing the topic.

"Much better. She misses you and so do the others. Carl's growing more every day."

"I . . . miss them too."

"Do . . . did you miss me?" he asked starkly.

He sounded so unsure of himself, so confused that finding the words to tell him everything that was on her mind was impossible. Instead she shook her head vigorously.

"I know that I've made some bad mistakes. . . . I know that I haven't any right to ask you to reconsider the divorce, but I love you, Caroline, and I'll do whatever you want to make things right between us again."

"I know," she said miserably.

"If you know that, then why are you acting like my being here is all wrong? It's that Larry fellow, isn't it? You've started seeing him again, haven't you?"

"Yes . . . no. We went to one movie and I cried through the entire comedy because I was so miserable without you. Finally Larry told me to get smart and go back to you where I belonged."

"He told you that?"

She nodded again.

"Is it Alaska, love? Would you rather we lived elsewhere?"

"No," she said quickly. "I love Alaska. It was the fever and the exhaustion and everything else that caused me to believe otherwise. You were right—a week after I arrived here I knew Seattle would never be my home again. My home is with you."

"Oh, love, I've been stir-crazy without you. Nothing is good anymore unless you're there to share it with me." Although it was awkward in the front seat of the car, Paul gathered her in his arms and kissed her with the hunger of a five-week absence. His mouth moved over hers slowly, sensuously, as though he couldn't believe she was in his arms and he half feared she'd disappear.

Caroline wrapped her arms around his neck and kissed him back with all the passion of the lonely weeks. Tears dampened her face and she buried her nose in his throat, heaving a sigh. "There's something you should know."

"What's that, love?"

"I . . . I didn't write the letter."

He went still. "What letter?"

"The one that told you I was pregnant."

Caroline could feel the air crack with electricity. The calm before the storm; the peace before the fury; the stillness before the outrage. She squeezed her eyes closed, waiting.

"You're not pregnant?"

"I swear I didn't know my aunts had written to you. I can only apologize. If you want, I . . ."

"Love." His index finger under her chin raised her gaze to his. "I didn't receive any letter."

"You . . . What? No letter?"

"None."

"You mean . . . Oh, Paul, Paul," she squeezed his neck and spread kisses that tasted of salt over his face. She kissed his eyes, his nose, his forehead, his chin and his mouth.... Again and again she ministered to his mouth until they were both winded and exhilarated.

"I didn't ever think I'd be thanking the postal service for their bi-weekly delivery," Paul said, and chuckled.

"You love me more than Diane." She said it with wonder, as though even now she wasn't sure it could possibly be true.

"Of course, love. You're my wife."

"But..."

"Diane was a long time ago."

"But you saved things to remember her by?"

"Only her letter. She decided she wasn't the type to live in the wilds of Alaska. She said that if I loved her, I'd be willing to give up this craziness and come to her."

"But why keep the letter?"

"To remind me that it takes a special kind of person to appreciate the challenge of Alaska. The land's not right for every woman, but it's right for you, love."

"Because you're right for me." Her face shone with her love. She was incredibly happy.

"I can't promise you that there won't be fevers, but I vow that I'll never leave you to face them alone and I'll never doubt you again."

"Nor I you." She felt like singing and dancing and loving this man until "his socks were turned inside out." She placed her head on his shoulder and sighed. "Can we go home soon? I miss Atta."

"Yes, love. Whenever you want."

"Is today too soon? Oh, Paul, I had the most marvelous idea about getting some additional medical training so that we could open a clinic."

"Love," he chuckled. "I sent for a mail-order bride, not a doctor."

"But I could have done so much more when the fever broke out if I'd had the proper supplies."

Paul's hand slipped under her sweater to caress her midriff. "I have a feeling you're going to be too preoccupied for quite some time to be thinking about doing any studying."

"But I can, can't I?"

"Yes, love. Anything you want."

"Oh, Paul, the only thing I want or need is you. Thank you for loving me, thank you for coming for me, and thank you for Scrabble."

"No, love," he said seriously. "Thank you."

With a happy, excited laugh, she hungrily placed her mouth over his.

*   *   *   *   *

He could torment her days with doubts
and her nights with desires that fired her soul.

Ride the Eagle

VITA VENDRESHA

He was everything she ever wanted. But they were opponents in
a labor dispute, each fighting to win. Would she risk her brilliant
career for the promise of love?

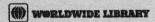

In response
to last year's outstanding success,
Silhouette Brings You:

Silhouette Christmas Stories 1987

Specially chosen for you in a delightful volume celebrating the holiday season, four original romantic stories written by four of your favorite Silhouette authors.

Dixie Browning—*Henry the Ninth*
Ginna Gray—*Season of Miracles*
Linda Howard—*Bluebird Winter*
Diana Palmer—*The Humbug Man*

Each of these bestselling authors will enchant you with their unforgettable stories, exuding the magic of Christmas and the wonder of falling in love.

A heartwarming Christmas gift during the holiday season...indulge yourself and give this book to a special friend!

Available November 1987

XM87-1